THE PARTY'S OVER

Bolan stepped into the room, raising his SMG to sweep the soldiers sitting at the bar.

His targets went down in a row, like ducks in a shooting gallery. Bolan used one hand to brace himself, vaulting the bar and dropping out of sight before the Triads at the tables could react. A barrage of pistol shots flew overhead, some of the bullets smashing liquor bottles on the shelves behind the bar. The Executioner stayed low and powered toward the gaming room, some forty feet in front of him, a frag grenade already in his hand. He dropped the pin and held the safety spoon in place, prepared to make the pitch as soon as he was satisfied no innocent civilians were inside the room.

Some of the players were emerging as he reached the far end of the bar. Bolan fired a short burst one-handed, dropping two in their tracks and driving the rest out of sight.

Don't start with me, boys, he thought. I came to play.

MACK BOLAN ®
The Executioner

DON PENDLETON'S
THE EXECUTIONER®
TARGET LOCK

A GOLD EAGLE BOOK FROM
WORLDWIDE.

TORONTO • NEW YORK • LONDON
AMSTERDAM • PARIS • SYDNEY • HAMBURG
STOCKHOLM • ATHENS • TOKYO • MILAN
MADRID • WARSAW • BUDAPEST • AUCKLAND

First edition May 2000
ISBN 0-373-64258-X

Special thanks and acknowledgment to
Mike Newton for his contribution to this work.

TARGET LOCK

Tyranny is always better organized than freedom.
                                    —Charles Péguy

To renounce liberty is to renounce
being a man, to surrender the rights
of humanity and even its duties.
                                    —Rousseau

I can't promise anyone liberty or even security,
but I can help them fight for what they need.
And sometimes, that's enough.
                                    —Mack Bolan

For Gunnery Sgt. Carlos Hathcock II,
the *real* Executioner: 93 registered kills in Vietnam,
plus a Silver Star for valor in the rescue of seven
wounded comrades on 16 September 1969.
R.I.P. 25 February 1999.

Prologue

Barely six months in Panama, and Philip Hong was sick of it already. He found fault with everything: the climate and the jungle, which reminded him of journeys to the Golden Triangle; the food, which turned his bowels to water; and the people, who impressed him as a band of savages so primitive, they should have lived in caves or small thatched huts.

He hated Panama, but couldn't leave. The master of his Triad had selected Hong particularly for his skill in moving drugs from one point to the next across hostile frontiers. Hong was compelled by honor and by threat of agonizing death to do as he was told, but there was nothing in his Triad oath that said he had to like it.

When Hong considered his assignment—which was often—he inevitably blamed the Portuguese. If they hadn't agreed to the surrender of Macau, Hong and his Triad brothers wouldn't have been driven from their homes by Beijing agents, wouldn't have been cut loose to drift around the world in search of sanctuary, someplace they could put down roots and prosper once again.

Of course, it hadn't truly been that sudden. Years had passed between the signing of a treaty for reversion of Macau to Red Chinese control and the event itself. Hong's master had been busy in the meantime buying friends, preparing for the day when they would have to leave their homeland. And through the master's wisdom, they had prospered...even if the tropic climate made Hong feel the need to shower several times each day.

This afternoon, miles from the nearest shower, hopelessly removed from any hint of air-conditioning, Hong occupied the shotgun seat of a U.S. Army surplus jeep, scowling as his driver made an effort to hit every rut and pothole on the unpaved, winding mountain track. The forest pressed in close on both sides of them, lush and green from near-constant rainfall on the slopes of the Serrania del Darién. The Colombian border was perhaps two miles behind them. If the shipment was in danger they could be attacked at any time.

In fact, two other shipments from Colombia had been ambushed, near this very spot, within the past six weeks. Because the trucks and their white cargo had been burned instead of stolen, there was some confusion as to who might be responsible for the attacks. Not Panamanian authorities, Hong knew, for they had been well paid to close their eyes. Not the Americans, for while their war on drugs continued, they had shown no further tendency to clean up Panama once Manuel Noriega had been kidnapped and imprisoned in the States.

So, who was left?

Hong ruled out rival traffickers, who would have surely stolen the cocaine, instead of burning it. Even the local peasants knew enough to grab a fortune when it fell in their laps. Destruction of the cargo, and the execution of his transport teams, meant something else entirely. The attacks were more than simple hazards of the modern narco trade.

They were deliberate acts of war.

Which helped explain why Philip Hong was riding in a U.S. Army surplus jeep, an AK-47 automatic rifle braced across his lap, waiting for a band of total strangers to attack him with homicidal intent. It explained why the cargo was different this time, a little surprise for the raiders. Some payback for the damage they had caused, thus far.

Hong had tried to explain that his personal presence in the convoy was superfluous, even foolhardy, but the master of his Triad was insistent. Hong was too intelligent to argue, knowing he had jeopardized his image in the master's eyes by merely suggesting he should remain in Panama City and coordinate the action from the safety of his own high-rise apartment. To reject the order outright would be nothing short of suicide, and if he had to die this day, Hong much preferred a bullet in the brain to what the master devised for subjects who defied him.

There was still a chance, Hong realized, that nothing might transpire. Although two shipments had been lost, three others had passed without incident over the same ground. Which meant that if they weren't attacked this afternoon, Hong would be forced to ride shotgun on one convoy after another until the issue was resolved.

Hong's scowl deepened, carving furrows in his cheeks. He craved a cigarette but wouldn't let himself become distracted from his mission, even for a moment. If he had to be there he would do the job as it should have been done the first time out, to meet the raiders and destroy them.

After all, there was no rule forbidding Philip Hong from taking pleasure in his work, however minimal that pleasure might turn out to be. He still enjoyed a killing, now and then, though he had risen through the Triad ranks—or thought he had before this latest trouble—to a point where others did his killing for him. It struck him as somehow fitting: where better to revert and spill the blood of enemies than in a savage, primitive environment like this?

It was like going on safari, Hong decided. A vacation to the wilds of Africa or Borneo. Instead of shooting tigers, leopards or gorillas he was engaged in hunting men. Armed men, at that, who had already killed several of his Triad brothers, thus incurring righteous fury that would stalk them to their graves.

Hong had an oath to keep and he didn't intend to let his master down, wouldn't disgrace himself by turning tail and running in the heat of combat, even if it meant his death.

Get on with it, he thought, and clutched the rifle in his lap more tightly, as he waited for the fun to start.

GUILLERMO CRUZ wasn't a violent man by nature, but his innate squeamishness hadn't prevented him from killing two men in the past six weeks. One of the men had been Chinese, the other Panamanian, and they were both his enemies. Both were involved, before their sudden deaths, in smuggling narcotics into Panama for shipment to the United States and Canada. For that offense, they had been tried, convicted and condemned.

Guillermo Cruz had no official status with the government of Panama. In fact, he hoped and prayed the government had no idea that he existed, though that hope was faint. More realistically, he kept his fingers crossed that agents for the state secret police didn't suspect his link to the resistance movement that had sprung up after Manuel Noriega was removed from power. The pledge to halt the traffic in narcotics and the general state of government corruption had largely been untouched since the American surgical strike of Operation Just Cause.

Cruz's shift from peaceful protest to guerrilla warfare had been gradual, a product of repression, time spent in a stinking cell with rats and lice for company, and the dawning recognition that his government was riddled with corruption from the presidential palace to the army private in his barracks to the policemen on patrol in squalid barrios. He realized nothing would change through free elections, since there were no free elections. All the fraud and violence practiced under Noriega had continued in his absence, but without protest from Washington. The other dealings carried out behind the facade of free enterprise had somehow managed to elude the U.S. State Department and the CIA—or else, the men who mattered in *El Norte* had decided to abandon Panama and leave the tiny nation to her fate.

Which left Cruz and those who shared his principles of liberty, integrity, and honor to defend their homeland by themselves. Beginning with the drug traffickers who continued moving poison through the country, bound for the United States and other First World markets.

Cruz wasn't concerned about Americans, Canadians or Europeans who defiled themselves with drugs. At thirty-two, he had elected to pick up the gun because narcotics traffic damaged Panama, his native land, in three distinct and separate ways. It fostered odious corruption in the government, thereby promoting sundry other crimes, malfeasances and harshly repressive measures to protect the outlaw trade. It granted foreigners—the narco traffickers—unhealthy influence in Panama when they should have been jailed, or at the very least deported on a rusty garbage scow. And finally, the narco traffic had made addicts of thousands of his countrymen, inevitably, as a portion of the deadly cargo found its way to native users, many of them hopeless peasants trapped in something close to feudalistic servitude, with no prospect for any joy in life, beyond the sweet oblivion of chemicals.

Cruz despised the men who brought this curse upon his homeland and if he couldn't pursue them in the courts—because they owned the legal system and the police—he would pursue their minions in the jungle, sap their strength one shipment at a time.

This attack would be their third. They had already burned two shipments—three truckloads of cocaine in the first, two in the second—and while Cruz had no idea how much the drug was worth in America, he knew they had stung the traffickers, perhaps even wounded them slightly. He knew that from the official reaction to the raids, military strikes against the nearest mountain villages in each case. Two dozen "suspects" were executed outright and at least a hundred more were hauled off to prison cells without even the pretext of a trial. He had considered calling off the next raid to prevent retaliation against the innocent, but his compatriots had voted to proceed.

And so they would.

The Thompson submachine gun that he carried was a vintage weapon, ranked obsolete by the Americans since the Korean War, but Cruz had no complaints about its ability. The other members of his strike team carried weapons ranging from old bolt-action rifles and double-barreled shotguns to M-16 A-2 assault rifles stolen from government arsenals. A rocket launcher or recoilless rifle would have been useful for stopping the trucks, but Cruz and his men would have to make do with what weapons they had...at least until one of their sympathizers in the army was able to arrange for heavier weapons to be "misplaced."

Still, for this action, he thought their equipment would do.

They had allowed the last three shipments to pass unmolested, Cruz overriding the protests of his comrades with simple logic. If they struck every convoy, became too predictable, they would be hunted down and killed in record time. This way, the uncertain progress of the attacks kept their enemies off balance, constantly nervous and expending vital cash and energy to double up the guard on every shipment, while the rebels stood back and bided their time. Then, when the drug traffickers had started to relax, the raiding would begin anew.

Cruz had no idea if they would be relaxed this soon, but he had felt compelled to strike again after four weeks of sitting on his hands. In part, it was standard operating procedure to allies who craved action, and who might desert him if they thought he had gone soft or lost his stomach for the fight. In equal part, though, Cruz despised the thought of letting one more shipment pass when they could take it out and thereby make the world at least a slightly better place.

He heard the convoy coming and raised a hand to signal the nearest of his comrades, trusting them to pass the signal on. None of them made a sound, although he doubted if their enemies could hear much over the sound of laboring engines. How many trucks, this time? How much cocaine?

How many men to kill?

He felt his stomach churning as it always did before the shooting started. Cruz didn't enjoy the killing, took no pleasure in it, but he knew what must be done. If the police and military chose to let the poison trade continue, unobstructed, someone else would have to fill the void and do their jobs for them, by any means available.

He cocked the Thompson, careful not to slip his index finger through the trigger guard until he had a target. They couldn't afford a clumsy accident when lives were riding on the line.

Another moment now. Another moment....

THE HELICOPTERS, like most other military gear in Panama, had been provided by the U.S. military, for a price. They were Sikorsky UH-60 Blackhawk gunships, each with three-man crews and a capacity for seating up to fourteen combat troops, with twin General Electric T-700 turboshaft engines cranking out 1,560 horsepower each, for a cruising speed of 167 miles per hour and an effective range of some 370 miles.

As one member of the selected twenty-eight combat troops, and their commander for the mission, Captain Luis

Perez should have been concerned about the adversaries they were stalking—numbers, skill and training, armament, the works. In truth, Captain Perez had no real worries, since his team was only meant to serve as backup if the convoy guards and Blackhawk crews left anyone alive.

All things considered, he didn't think that would be a problem. The convoy's security personnel were a mixed bag of Chinese Triad members, Colombian assassins and home-grown Panamanian thugs, all armed to the teeth. If they failed to repulse an attack on the motorcade, the twin Blackhawks were armed with pintle-mounted .50-caliber GECAL Gatling guns, plus wing-mounted M-20/19 rocket pods, each containing nineteen rockets, for a total of seventy-six per gunship. Finally, if any of the rebels managed to survive that dose of Hell on Earth, Captain Perez's men would hit the ground with their M-16/M203 combo rifle and grenade launcher, ready and able to mop up the ragtag survivors.

It would be, as one of the American advisors still in Panama had ventured to suggest, "a fucking turkey shoot." Captain Perez had never shot a turkey in his life, but he was looking forward to the new experience.

In truth, Perez had no grudge against the rebels who killed traffickers, especially if their victims were Chinese or Colombians, but he had orders to obey, a rank and pension to protect. He also stood to gain financially, if he impressed the men who had arranged this cooperative venture, teaming military forces with a band of felons who should certainly have been in prison, if not lined against a wall for execution by a firing squad.

Still, that was life in Panama. The government had been collaborating with assorted wealthy outlaws for so long that Perez, a relative youngster at thirty years old, had never known a better system. There had always been corruption in the military, backing one gangster or another in the presidential palace, ignoring the contraband trade for a price, while suppressing domestic dissent. After decades, of such service, what other function was the military even suited to perform?

The Blackhawks held position, circling at four thousand feet, some six miles north of where the convoy was laboriously bumping its way across the Serrania del Darién. The position had been calculated to avoid alerting any rebels in the neighborhood, while placing the gunships close enough to respond in seconds if they received word of an ambush. Three seconds, give or take, to reach the killing ground and rain destruction on their peasant enemies.

Captain Perez was mildly startled, then amused, to find that he was looking forward to it, hoping that the rebels would appear. He had a chance to distinguish himself, impress his superiors enough perhaps to take another step up the ladder of promotion, and to do a bit of hunting, all at the same time.

Perez was musing on the prospect when the radio crackled, his own headset picking up static at first, then an excited voice using their code name, Stallion, on the restricted military frequency. The caller spoke in halting Spanish, with an accent, but his message came through clear enough.

The trap had been sprung. If any proof was needed, gunfire in the background provided it, sharp and loud, like fireworks at a village festival.

"We go!" Perez informed his pilot, who echoed the order to the second Blackhawk as they broke the circling pattern, heading south along the ragged spine of mountains. They were on the scene almost before Perez could focus on the battleground below them.

The motorcade—a jeep in front, three covered trucks behind—had driven into a cross fire as it cleared a pass between two jutting slabs of stone. The ambush site had been an obvious choice, providing the attackers with both altitude and cover for themselves. The convoy guards were catching hell, but they were also standing fast, with no place to go if they gave up the cover of their vehicles.

"Attack!" Perez commanded. "And avoid the trucks."

That part of it was understood, of course, but Captain Perez wanted his last-minute order recorded, in case the Colombian cargo should suffer any incidental damage from friendly fire. It wouldn't be his fault, whatever happened next. He didn't fly the helicopter, after all, or aim the guns and rockets. Any accidental losses would be charged against the Blackhawk crews.

Perfect.

Captain Perez could sit back and enjoy the show.

They went in with the .50-caliber Gatlings first, one Blackhawk swooping low along each side of the trail, hosing the tree line and crags with a storm of automatic fire. It was impossible to see if any of the armor-piercing bullets found their mark. The rebels were too well hidden to be spotted on a single high-speed pass, but Perez saw tree trunks explode from the impact.

The gunships overflew their target zone and circled back, reversing sides, so that the Blackhawk that had sprayed the west side of the trail now took the east, and vice versa. On this pass, they gave the overheated Gatling guns a rest, each chopper unleashing perhaps a quarter of its 2.75-inch rockets into the forest flanking the road. The high-explosive warheads came equipped with impact fuzes, detonating as they struck earth, granite, trees—anything at all.

The woods were smoking, maybe burning, when the Blackhawks circled back for yet another pass. More rockets streaked into the forest like a storm of arrows launched by vengeful gods, erupting into gouts of yellow flame. Captain Perez could see the surviving convoy gunners crouching near their trucks, arms raised to shield their faces from the sudden rush of superheated air.

Perez found that he was smiling, a ferocious grin that strained the muscles in his cheeks until they twitched. It was a slaughterhouse down there. Another pass or two to clear the field, and he would lead his soldiers in to mop up any stray survivors of the rebel ambush team.

GUILLERMO CRUZ had almost canceled the ambush at the last moment, overwhelmed by a sudden sense of foreboding, but then the dusty jeep came into view, and it was too late to signal a retreat without exposing his men on the flanks to fire. He had no choice but to proceed and ignore the gnawing in his gut.

He didn't have to signal for the shooting to begin. They had arranged that in advance, agreeing that they'd allow the first three vehicles—assuming there were more than three—to clear the pass before they opened fire. A special squad of marksmen would attempt to stall the last truck by, blasting the tires, the engine block, whatever they could do to stop it cold and keep the vehicles in front of it from backing up. The other vehicles would be trapped then, forced to run the gauntlet of their guns until the drivers had been killed.

The first few seconds of the ambush seemed to go as Cruz had planned, his soldiers pouring fire into the drug convoy from both sides, snipers on the high ground making it a three-dimensional trap. He only had a dozen soldiers, but that still meant four guns for each vehicle, besides his own, and Cruz believed that they could do this job as they had done it twice before.

He fired a short burst from his Thompson toward the jeep and watched the heavy .45-caliber slugs knock shiny divots in the faded, dusty paint. It startled him, the sight of clean, bright metal underneath, but he wasn't distracted from his targets bailing out the other side.

Chinese. More Triads, come to pick his homeland clean

and make his people hopeless slaves to one drug or another. Bastards!

Cruz was sighting down the Thompson's barrel, hoping for a better shot when it happened. With a shout and a blaze of automatic weapons' fire, men started piling out of the two covered trucks, each man armed and firing toward the trees, the rocks, wherever snipers had concealed themselves.

Cruz tried to count them but gave up when he hit two dozen, understanding that the bastards had been ready for him. They were trying to spring a trap in reverse, outnumbering their enemy, but Cruz and his soldiers still held the superior position. They had cover, while the convoy's gunmen were exposed, a few of them already down and twitching in the mud, while others scrambled to hide beneath their trucks.

There could be no hiding behind the vehicles since Cruz had troops on both sides of the road. He fired another burst toward the nearest truck and saw a Chinese gunman stagger and fall, clutching his chest has crimson spilled out between his fingers. They could do it! They could turn the traffickers' trick around and send a message back to those who shipped the drugs.

This road is closed.

A smile was tugging at the corners of his mouth, just as he heard the helicopters. There was no mistaking, the *whop-whop* of their rotors overhead, and when the gunships came in firing at the trees Guillermo knew it was too much. The bastards had prepared their trap too well, and he had blundered into it.

Cruz shouted for his soldiers to retreat, to save themselves, but few of them could hear him with the battle raging all around.

The helicopters came in low in tandem, hosing the tree line on both sides of the trail with heavy machine-gun fire.

It was like nothing Cruz had ever seen or heard before, the guns so fast, so powerful. A bullet stuck the tree he crouched behind, perhaps a yard above his head, and he was stung by splinters from the mutilated trunk and the bark raining into his hair.

Cruz heard an anguished cry and glanced toward the sound, losing his focus on the convoy and the helicopters for a moment. On his left, perhaps twelve paces away, Paco Calderone was writhing on his back screaming, trying to stuff his entrails back inside his body, his blood-slick fingers failing at their task.

Cruz locked eyes with his dying soldier and he realized all of them were doomed. The knowledge galvanized him, fed his heart and brain a rush of something that would pass for courage, and he emptied out the Thompson's 30-round box magazine in one long burst, blowing the old jeep's tires and puncturing the gasoline can mounted close behind the driver's seat. His bullets struck a spark, and flames began to dance around the rear deck of the jecp before the fuel can blew like a king-sized Molotov cocktail.

Cruz was feeding the Thompson a fresh magazine when he heard the helicopters coming back. They weren't firing machine guns this time but had switched to rockets. The initial detonations rocked the earth beneath his feet, and Cruz was falling back before he even recognized the impulse to protect himself. He didn't think about his soldiers or the convoy, and while that would shame him later, at the moment all Guillermo Cruz could think of was himself, surviving to behold another day.

One of the rockets struck a tree off to his left, not far from where the bullets had found Paco Calderone. Perhaps the spot was cursed or maybe it was blind luck? Cruz saw the missile coming and saw the great tree shiver before it burst apart in smoke and flame. A branch roughly the thickness of his biceps struck Cruz on the shoulder, grazed his skull and knocked him sprawling on his back.

Somehow, he kept the Thompson when he fell. He regained his senses moments later when the wave of manmade thunderbolts had passed him by. He heard the helicopters coming back again and staggered to his feet, prepared to meet death like a man…but there was something different. The engine sounds had changed, somehow, and there was no incoming fire.

He blinked away the dirt and leaf mold from his eyes in time to see the gunships hovering a few feet off the ground, disgorging soldiers dressed in jungle camouflage. Cruz hesitated long enough to see that the arriving troops paid no attention to the Chinese gangsters or their trucks loaded with drugs. Instead, they formed two skirmish lines, each facing a side of the trail, and started jogging toward the trees.

Cruz broke and ran.

He heard the soldiers closing on him from behind, shouting directions back and forth, reporting when they stumbled onto corpses. Were his men all dead? Was he the last survivor of the raiding party?

Did it even matter, now?

A different kind of shout—excited, eager—told Cruz that they had seen him running through the forest. He could stand and fight, remembering what the troops had done to simple folk for years on end and take some of them with him, but he chose to keep running, straining for a bit more speed. When they began to fire at him, he swung the Tommy gun around one-handed and unleashed a ragged burst, not even glancing back to see if he hit anything.

If anyone had asked him earlier Cruz would have said he knew this land as well as any man, but when he reached the cliff it came as a complete surprise. Below him, some two hundred feet, a river snaked its way between the high-rise slabs of stone. He had a glimpse of ferns and stunted trees down there before the vertigo kicked in and forced him away from the brink.

Harsh voices were drawing closer. Someone was laughing at him. They had him cornered and they knew it. They could take their time killing him, use him for target practice if they felt like it. It was a game the soldiers of his country seemed to find amusing.

Furious, Guillermo Cruz turned back to face them as he braced the submachine gun at his hip and sprayed the forest with a last, long burst. The voices sounded angry now, or maybe even worried.

Better.

There was no time to reload before they reached him and their bullets cut him down. Cruz had a choice to make, and literally no time to consider it.

Still clinging to the empty Thompson, he turned and approached the brink once more, sized up the drop...and stepped into the air.

1

There are many worse places to work undercover than Panama City. The town itself was Third World all the way, with beggars on the streets, slums to rival any found in Latin America and streets unsafe at any hour. Still, English is spoken virtually everywhere, and white skin doesn't rate a second glance, except from thieves or would-be tour guides.

Mack Bolan didn't feel at home in Panama—indeed, he seldom had that feeling anywhere—but he was more or less at ease. Considering the high-risk nature of his mission, Bolan felt remarkably relaxed, in fact. He hadn't flown commercial, so his bags hadn't been searched upon departure, and the Customs agents who were waiting for him on arrival obviously didn't give a damn what kind of contraband was brought into their country. Bolan guessed that it would be a different story going out, when there was money to be made by overlooking anything from drugs to pre-Columbian antiquities, but he wasn't concerned about departure rituals just now.

The main thing had been getting all his military hardware into Panama. Whatever managed to survive his visit could be left behind. It was expendable.

And so, in fact, was he.

It didn't bother Bolan, knowing that he had been dropped into the middle of an economically depressed, politically unstable powder keg. If anything, that was the very quality that made him feel the most at home. He had grown up with danger, violence and intrigue in one jungle or another, with enemies whose faces changed but whose techniques were always similar. The predators ran true to form, because they had no choice. They simply knew no other way to live—or die.

Four hours on the ground and he had used up half that time to learn his way around the city, checking out the so-called "safe" apartment that had been waiting for him, courtesy of Hal Brognola's contacts in the CIA. He didn't plan on spending much time there, and while part of that decision sprang from his desire to finish his job as rapidly as possible, he also harbored a mistrust of any favors from the Company. Experience had taught him that there was no rule of thumb for judging spooks. Living lies and trading secrets on a daily basis challenged the integrity of any man or woman, and too many were unequal to the task.

This brought his thoughts back to the man he was supposed to meet. A "friend," he had been told before he left the States. That could mean anything or nothing, when the chips were down. Assuming that the man was what he claimed to be—a patriot who wanted help flushing out some of the slime that had infested Panama in recent years, and help to block the increase of drugs bound for America. Bolan had faced his share of hopeless odds before and had managed to survive, but he didn't delude himself that he could clean up Panama in one short visit, much less if he had to fight alone.

And if it came down to a kamikaze mission, he would cut his losses while he had the chance. Do what he could to get the ball in play, before he caught the next flight out and wished the local players well.

The man known as the Executioner wasn't afraid of death, but he wasn't suicidal either. He would gladly risk his life, surrender it if necessary, in the proper cause, but he wasn't about to fall in some futile gesture that was doomed before he even made his move.

Assessment of the situation was his first priority, and there had been no way for him to render vital judgments from the safety of *El Norte*, as the USA was known most everywhere below the Rio Grande. He had to judge the situation for himself, check out the players and the odds, before deciding if it was a game worth dying for.

Step one was touching base with his connection and reputed ally in Panama City, hearing the story firsthand, without interpreters to edit or elaborate. If Brognola's report checked out, and Bolan felt that he could trust the locals, then he would proceed with the engagement, one step at a time. It would be complicated and dangerous, with no guarantee of his survival, much less victory. That didn't trouble Bolan, though. He simply had to know there was a fighting chance.

He had an address for his contact, in addition to the scheduled rendezvous. A part of checking out this friend whom he had never met was showing up ahead of time and shadowing thek guy en route to keep their blind date at a downtown restaurant. The tail would give him time to check out his contact, see whether he made any stops along the way and find out if he was traveling alone. It was an inexpensive kind of life insurance, making sure this total stranger didn't have an ambush waiting for the gringo warrior he had ordered up like room service to help him fight his war.

Why would he orchestrate an ambush? Sitting in his rented car across the street, a half block down, Bolan could think of several reasons. First and foremost, it was possible the whole thing was a setup, start to finish, engineered by someone in the Company who nursed a grudge against Brognola or the team at Stony Man Farm, in Virginia. Brognola's private army had clashed with the spooks more than once, rooting out traitors in the process, and some victories were never forgiven or forgotten.

On the other hand, it was entirely possible that Brognola's connection in the CIA was clean, but may have been misled by someone on the ground in Panama. A setup by the triads, maybe, or by someone in the paramilitary clique that schemed and plotted for a rerun of the "good old days" when uniforms ran Panama and worked the population almost as a captive labor force. How much had changed since Noriega fell besides the faces at the top?

Bolan picked out his contact when the man emerged from the run-down apartment house, downrange. He recognized the stranger's profile from the snapshots he had memorized. He reached for the ignition key as his connection started walking north. Five seconds later, Bolan knew another fact about the man who was supposed to be his ally.

Friend or foe, the guy was being tailed—by someone else.

"IT'S HIM!" Ismael Ramirez said. None of the others answered, of course. They recognized the target and didn't need Ramirez's help to pick him out, especially when there was no one else in sight.

Ramirez was embarrassed by the blunder born of eagerness, but the embarrassment turned instantly to anger. He could feel the warm flush in his face and was conscious of his sudden death grip on the Argentine FMK-3 submachine gun he held in his lap.

The weapon was a cheap but effective variant of the Israeli Uzi and the Czech vz 23, chambered in 9 mm Parabellum, with a 40-round box magazine inserted through the pistol grip. From where he sat, some thirty feet behind his target with an unobstructed view, Ramirez could have killed the man easily, cut him down in his tracks and left him to bleed out on the sidewalk as he had done to at least a dozen other victims.

Unfortunately, he had orders to capture the traitor alive, deliver him for interrogation to a certain address on the waterfront. He could guess what would happen from there and Ramirez, for his part, would have preferred a merciful bullet to the back of the head. Still, that was none of his concern. The only thing he had to worry about was failure and the price of bungling a simple snatch-and-grab assignment.

Antonio was at the wheel, all business, hunched forward as if he was preparing to drive the Grand Prix for a purse in the millions of dollars. The grin on his face might have been eagerness, or plain stupidity. With Antonio, it was often difficult to tell, but the youth knew how to drive. There was no mistake about that.

In the back seat, Jorge and Jesus were armed with pistols to intimidate their target if he felt like fighting, but they weren't supposed to use their weapons. Ramirez had driven that point home repeatedly, harping on it until the others rolled their eyes and repeated the words while he spoke, making fun. In other circumstances, Ramirez might have slapped them, daring either one of them to challenge his authority, but at the moment he required their full cooperation, no sulking when the time came to leap from the car and drag their target back by sheer force. He needed them alert and willing, even if intelligent was too much to hope for.

The assignment had come down to him the night before without warning, leaving little time for Ramirez to pick soldiers. He had used what was available, trusting Jorge and Jesus as far as he could see them. And that was all that mattered since they wouldn't be left alone on this mission or trusted to think for themselves.

It was a shame, Ramirez sometimes thought, that the

death squad couldn't recruit a better class of personnel. Still, what could he expect? The bulk of those who joined were former soldiers and policemen, well below the usual retirement age. There was a reason they were separated from their uniforms, beyond the mere corruption or brutality of which they stood accused when they were fired. The crime wasn't in taking bribes or cracking heads, per se; it was in getting caught, being so clumsy at their trade that their own corrupt superiors couldn't afford to look the other way. So they were stupid going in and those who came to the death squad without a background in the army or police work were no more than common street thugs, mouthing patriotic slogans as they sought a way to carry on their crimes without the risk of being sent to prison.

They were scum.

Ismael Ramirez sometimes wondered where he fit into the scheme of things, how he compared to those who were his nominal subordinates. He, too, had been cashiered from the security police, though he had managed to attain a higher rank—lieutenant—than the other men who served him now. His error had been patriotic fervor, gunning down three dissidents after a demonstration in the city's reeking barrio. He was unaware of the television camera following him until it was too late. His second error had been failing to retrieve the camera and tape, destroy them both, along with the camera. Though it wasn't for lack of trying. He had simply lost the bastard in a foot pursuit twice firing at the younger man in haste and missing him both times.

Stupid.

But he was still a patriot who understood his duty, and was thankful for a chance to put things right, to compensate for his mistake. If he no longer wore the uniform that once made him so proud, at least he was permitted to continue fighting, beating back the dissidents and scum who threatened to subvert his homeland and his way of life.

"Get after him!" Ramirez snapped, Antonio responding with a grunt that sounded like a hog inhaling slop. The engine chugged and sputtered, finally responding to the twist of the ignition key, Ramirez had to slap Antonio for stealing a defective car. Between seventy-five and one hundred cars were stolen each day in Panama City alone and, while most of those were cannibalized for parts or sold on the thriving black market, a fair number were taken for use in more serious crimes: night raids conducted by the death squads; kidnappings for ransom by a score of active gangs; bank robberies and other crimes committed by a ragtag list of rebels ranging from the far right to the revolutionary left. Auto theft was a new growth industry in Panama, and Ramirez saw no irony or hypocrisy in the fact that death squads sometimes executed car thieves, invariably driving the miscreants to their execution sites in stolen cars.

Antonio was driving like a damned old woman, creeping up behind the target almost as if afraid of overtaking him. Ramirez understood the strategy. It was intended to avoid spooking the target, putting him to flight, but he was anxious to get on with it. The longer they delayed, the greater risk of witnesses appearing on the scene, their target ducking down an alleyway or disappearing into yet another of the cheap apartment houses lining both sides of the street.

"Catch up, for God's sake!"

Antonio accelerated in response to his command. Ramirez heard and felt one of his knuckles pop, as he tightened his grip on the submachine gun. If it had been a plastic replica he would have crushed it in his callused hands. As it was, his palms felt greasy, slick with perspiration. He wiped them on his trousers, one after the other, his fingers aching when he forced them to release the weapon in his lap.

No shooting, he repeated to himself. Just grab the bastard. Take him to the waterfront.

It wasn't often that he was required to bring a subject in alive, of course. The group he served was called a death squad for a reason. It specialized in executions, frequently involving torture and postmortem mutilation of the corpse to make a point with friends or criminal associates of the deceased. Abductions were typically preludes to the execution and it made no lasting difference if the target suffered fatal injuries before they got him in the car.

This time was different, though. Ismael Ramirez had his orders, and it didn't take a rocket scientist to know who would be held responsible if anything went wrong. As team leader, he bore the ultimate responsibility, and if his masters wanted this pig in one piece to question him at leisure then Ramirez must not disappoint them.

If he failed, the next time he went cruising in a stolen car, it might turn out to be a one-way ride.

As they were about to overtake the target, Ramirez twisted in his seat to glare at Jorge and Jesus. "Alive!" he snapped. "Remember that. Make no mistakes."

"*Sí, sí,*" Jesus responded, wearily. Jorge just blinked at him and smiled, the idiot.

Another moment, and Antonio was standing on the brakes, cranking the wheel toward the curb. Behind Ramirez, his two soldiers vaulted from the stolen car and raced across the pavement toward their prey.

HE WOKE EACH MORNING in surprise to find that he was still alive. It was incongruous to him, with so many others having died, that he should live on and walk the streets like any other man untouched by death.

They would be hunting him, of course. That much was obvious, and it was yet another reason why each sunrise that he witnessed startled him. In general, the death squads were believed to be exceedingly efficient. Throughout Panama they had a reputation similar, albeit more grotesque, to that of the Royal Canadian Mounted Police. The death squads always got their man. Or woman. Sometimes children. Size and gender made no difference; the death squads never missed.

So why was he still alive?

It wasn't that he yearned for death, though he had moments when the weight of all the young men he had led to early graves pressed upon him, threatening to crush his spirit flat and squeeze out the last drop of humanity. In dreams he saw their faces, smiling first, then twisted into screams of agony.

So many faces.

When he awoke from such a dream, while he was waiting for his pulse to stabilize, he would remind himself that he wasn't the man responsible for all those deaths. He simply spoke of freedom and the right of patriots to take their homeland back from those who bored their way inside like termites, undermining the foundations of a civilized society, corrupting everything they touched. If men of character responded to his words, his writings, then it was his job—his duty—to direct their energies, help them to recognize their enemies and act, before the evil twins of fear and apathy crept up behind them and stole their courage.

So many lives.

But he wasn't the man who had imported truckloads of narcotics, turning Panama into a major transit point for drugs en route to the United States. He hadn't welcomed foreigners, including the Chinese and the Colombians, to wipe their filthy boots on the Panamanian flag, leaving bloody tracks all over the country. He wasn't the one who had made addicts of thousands of his countrymen, intimidated, brutalized or murdered many thousands more.

He simply tried to stop these evil things from happening, to put them right. For this, they hunted him, and would continue until he died.

One thing they wouldn't do was drive him from his homeland. Others had escaped, preferring exile from their families and friends to murder in the dead of night, and while he didn't judge them for their choice, he wouldn't run. The hunters would inevitably track him down but they wouldn't find him in Mexico or the United States or France. When they caught up to him, when they were finished with their knives and ice picks and electric prods, he would be buried in the plot where other members of his family had gone to rest for the past hundred years.

Unless the killers dumped his body in the jungle for the animals to feast upon. Unless they buried him at sea. Unless…

No matter. Even if they sealed his corpse inside a trunk and shipped it to Japan, the bastards would still know that they had never made him run.

Hiding…well, that was something else. That was most certainly allowed. In fact, he had been hiding for the past five weeks, another fact that made him question the alleged omniscience of the mighty death squads. He had never even left the city, though his comrades in the movement had assisted him by spreading tales that he was seen in Tucutí, in Chepo, and as far west as Gualaca. It amused him in his lighter moments to imagine hit teams prowling through the streets of towns where he hadn't set foot in years, if ever, sweating under bulky coats they wore to hide their weapons, cursing God and those who gave them their orders when they came up empty, once again.

He saw the humor in it, but it never lasted long. Each time he made them look like idiots, another mark was drawn against his name. There would be that much more to answer for when they caught up to him at last.

With any luck, he thought, it wouldn't be today.

The sun was warm upon his face as he emerged from the piss-stained lobby of the cheap apartment house. The day would be another hot one, muggy, with a dash of rain in the afternoon if they were lucky. It was a risk simply to step outside but he had work to do, a rendezvous to keep.

With the American.

He hadn't taken to the whole idea, at first. Historically, America was part of the problem in Panama, not the solution. It galled him to ask help from the same people who had first installed Manuel Noriega in the presidential palace, then dragged him out in chains and finally replaced him with an equally corrupt regime, which had refined the process of oppression with a few new twists.

He knew, of course, why the Americans were willing to assist him now. They were afraid of the Chinese. The Cold War might be over, insofar as television commentators were concerned, and China might attain "most favored nation" status in its commerce with *El Norte,* but Beijing and Washington would always be at odds, unless the Chinese mimicked Moscow and renounced the system they had struggled to promote for over half a century. Meanwhile, Chinese encroachment in the western hemisphere was bound to get a rise out of the cloak-and-dagger types in the United States.

It was his only card and he had played it boldly, spelling out the threat in no uncertain terms. He had been disappointed when he learned the Yanks were only sending one man to assist him but his contact had assured him it would be a very special man, a warrior unsurpassed.

Big talk. He would believe it when he saw results, but in the meantime there was nothing he could do but keep their rendezvous, trying his best to reach the downtown restaurant on time—and alive.

He heard the screech of tires a moment later, felt his scrotum shrivel as he turned and saw the dark sedan stop in the middle of the street. There were four men inside and two of them were leaping out with pistols in their hands.

He wasted precious microseconds wondering if he should run or fight, deciding they would gun him down in either case if they couldn't force him inside the car.

He had a Walther P5 pistol tucked inside his belt, against his spine, but he had never been a quick-draw artist and he stood no chance against two men with weapons drawn, already pointed at his chest.

So be it, then. At least, he wouldn't let them carry him away and torture him for days on end.

He turned and bolted, waiting for the bullet that would drill him through the back and bring him down.

BOLAN WAS READY when the shooters made their move. He had been trailing in the rental car since they had tipped their hand and started following the man he was supposed to meet. Beside him, close at hand, was his Beretta 93-R pistol with the custom sound suppressor and 20-round extended magazine, its fire selector set for 3-round bursts.

He reckoned it would be enough, unless the gunners had on some kind of body armor beneath their baggy shirts. It didn't look that way but, just in case, he had a second weapon ready on the empty shotgun seat. It was a Desert Eagle semiauto pistol, chambered in .44 Magnum, loaded with eight Teflon-coated rounds. The press at home called them "cop killers," but bullets were blind to their targets, and these would punch through Kevlar as if it were simple denim.

Just in case.

He saw the flare of brake lights, two men leaping from the back seat of the dark sedan, both brandishing pistols. Their sudden onslaught clearly took the target by surprise. Bolan's contact hesitated for a vital moment, then spun on his heel and started sprinting up the street, away from Bolan and the hit team.

They would kill him now, if that was all they wanted,

and Bolan couldn't do a thing about it. He was still too far away, although closing fast. Instead of shooting he saw the gunmen take off running after their intended victim, trailed by the sedan, and he experienced a sudden flash of hope. If they were set on capturing the man alive, he had a fighting chance.

Standing on the accelerator, Bolan overtook the chase car after thirty yards or so, then cranked his wheel and slammed on the brakes to cut them off. He bailed out on the driver's side, with the Beretta in his right hand and the Desert Eagle in his left, ready for anything. Before all hell broke loose, he saw his contact flick a hasty glance in his direction, frowning, a confused expression on his face. He had no time to concentrate on that as the shooters on the sidewalk swung around to face him, pistols tracking into target acquisition.

The Executioner chose the gunner on his right, for no reason other than convenience, and stroked the Beretta's trigger, slamming three rounds of 9 mm Parabellum ammo into the target's chest. He had a vague impression of the shooter going over backward, crimson splashed across his shirt—no body armor, then—before he framed the second target in his sights and fired a second 3-round burst.

The dying gunman staggered, clutching at his chest, and triggered off a wild round of his own. It smashed a window on the far side of the street and never came within a dozen yards of Bolan. By the time his second kill lay facedown on the sidewalk, the soldier had already turned to face the two surviving members of the snatch team, still in the sedan.

The driver seemed hell-bent on getting out of there, grinding the gears into reverse, but Bolan beat him to it, triggering a Desert Eagle thunderclap from twenty feet away. The bullet punched a golf ball-sized hole in the sedan's windshield and kept going, striking the driver above one eye, painting the back seat red, with chunky flecks of gray and white.

That left one shooter, and he wasn't going anywhere unless he fled on foot. Bolan was ready when he crawled out of the car and crouched behind his open door for cover, firing underneath it with some kind of compact submachine gun. Wild bullets rattled off the asphalt, a couple of them striking Bolan's rental car by accident, scarring the bumper and the trunk.

Enough.

The Desert Eagle spoke again, two shots so close together that the second sounded like an instant echo of the first. An armored car might have resisted them, but not a four-year-old Toyota Celica. The Teflon rounds punched through and found flesh. Bolan's adversary lurched into the open gasping like a stranded fish, the muzzle of his SMG describing crazy circles in the air.

A 3-round burst from the Beretta 93-R put him down, heels drumming on the pavement as the gunner's life spilled out into a spreading crimson pool. His weapon clattered in the street, dead fingers giving up their grip.

Bolan was grim-faced as he turned to scan the sidewalk for his contact, certain that he would have done the smart thing, kept running and to hell with any rendezvous downtown. His premature arrival might have saved the stranger's life, but it had also blown his chance of keeping their appointment and obtaining information he would need to judge if he should stay and fight or say goodbye and catch the next flight home.

He was surprised, therefore, to see the man crouched inside a recessed doorway near the intersection just ahead. He had stopped to watch the fight instead of fleeing while he had the chance.

And now, he had a small pistol in his hand.

"You want to use that," Bolan said in English. "Now would be the time."

His contact rose and stepped into the open, glancing at the dead men on the sidewalk. He didn't point the gun at Bolan, but he kept it in his hand.

"You are American," he said.

"And you," the Executioner replied, "must be Guillermo Cruz."

2

Forty-two hours earlier, before the guns went off in Panama City, Mack Bolan had walked with his second oldest living friend among the snow-white markers in Arlington National Cemetery. Surrounded by monuments to the heroic dead, he had listened intently while Hal Brognola asked him to risk his life. Again.

"You're wondering why Panama?" The director of Sensitive Operations said, though Bolan hadn't voiced the question. "I'm guessing, if you picked a hundred people off the street at random, none of them could tell you what's been happening down there since Noriega took his fall. A few of them would probably remember that complete control of the canal reverts to Panama this year, under the treaty Jimmy Carter signed, but for the rest of it—" Brognola snapped his fingers and dismissed the notion with a small, limp-wristed wave "—forget about it."

"So, why don't you fill me in," the Executioner replied.

"We've got two problems down in Panama," Brognola said. "One problem—drugs shipped through to the United States—has actually gotten worse since Noriega went to jail. Who would've figured that? Instead of just Colombian cocaine, they're also moving tons of China white. I mean that literally, by the way. Tons of the shit is getting through."

The big Fed paused a moment, then continued. "Which brings us to our second problem, and a new one for the region—the Chinese. Were you aware that they've moved into Panama in force?''

"I must have missed it," Bolan said.

"Yeah," Brognola retorted. "So did everybody else— as in *the New York Times, the Wall Street Journal*, Katie Couric, Peter Jennings, *USA Today*—pick any mouthpiece for the so-called news media you want to name and this is one event they haven't covered. Not a freaking word.''

The soldier knew better than to push his friend. Brognola had a point and he would get around to it when he was finished venting steam. The media was known to tick him off almost as much as judges who sentenced repeat offenders to house arrest or probation. The big Fed regarded the whole fourth estate, with one or two isolated exceptions, as a mob of trendy sycophants who valued ratings over honesty and who would kiss a psycho-killer's backside for the sake of an exclusive prime-time interview.

"Long story short," Brognola said at last, "the Chinese have been moving into Panama since 1991. Hard-liners in the States were worried that the Carter treaty might have opened up a door for Russia, but they missed the call. Instead of branching out, the USSR fell apart and left the field wide open for their chief competitors. Of course, Beijing knows that we'd never stand for Chinese troops in Panama, so they came up with something different.''

"Let me guess," Bolan replied. "The corporate approach?''

"Bingo!" the man from Washington replied. "Assorted Chinese companies—which means, of course, the Chinese government—have purchased giant tracts of real estate in Panama at bargain-basement rates. One outfit, the Panama Harbor Authority, presently controls traffic through *all* of Panama's major ports on both coasts and north and south. When we pull out the last of our troops, it will also control the canal, lock, stock and barrel. The Panama Harbor Authority, incidentally, is a recognized front for the Chinese military.''

Bolan frowned at that, recognizing the potential strategic threat to American interests in that scenario, with Red Chinese generals controlling access to the Panama Canal. In any given crisis situation, they could simply slam the door and lock it, barring passage of U.S. warships, or—in the alternative—challenging America to a display of force that would undoubtedly wring protests from the United Nations and the Organization of American States.

''They didn't see this coming at the State Department?'' Bolan asked.

''They see all kinds of things at State,'' Brognola said. ''But seeing and reacting are two different things. Remember, we've been dealing with the Chinese as a 'favored nation' for the past twelve years, and never mind Tiananmen Square. We've gone for trade agreements that subordinated human rights and sold them missile guidance systems that could drop ICBMs on Washington. It's frigging politics disguised as great diplomacy. Who wants to make a stink about the Panama Canal with all those nifty campaign contributions rolling in?''

''So, who's complaining now?'' asked Bolan.

''DEA, for one,'' Brognola said. ''And the U.S. Attorney General's office. Seems we've got another Chinese problem down in Canal Zone, which the gang at State just noticed.''

''That would be…?''

''The Triads,'' Brognola replied. ''You know about Macau reverting to the mainland government in 1999? Okay. The Portuguese pulled out with the agreement that Beijing would make no changes in the district's way of life for fifty years. Same deal with Hong Kong when the Brits bailed out a few three years ago. The Triads have good reason not to trust the Reds, of course. Too many of them saw the wrong side of a firing squad when Mao took over back in

'49 and they've been hounded from the country every time they try to get another toehold. That's one side of it, at least.''

"The other being heroin," added the soldier.

"Right as rain," Brognola said. "You know as well as anybody that the so-called Golden Triangle has never really been a triangle, at all. They grow as much opium in southern China as in Burma, Laos and Thailand put together, and the Triads have been selling it for decades, forking over a percentage of the income to Beijing. When they bailed out of Hong Kong and Macau, the Triads already had colonies in place around the world, from Canada to South America.''

"And Panama?" the Executioner suggested.

"Right, again. They pay their graft on time, and with the mainland Chinese buying up a hefty portion of the country, who's to gripe about some Chinese gangsters picking up the drug trade? They had deals in place with the Colombians, so now, along with the traditional cocaine shipments, they're moving high-grade heroin, as well. The local government's cut is twenty-five percent, and so's the Panamanian Harbor Authority. It makes Iran-Contra look like streetcorner dealing for some nickel bags.''

"That's it?"

"Don't I wish," Brognola said. "On top of everything, you've got the so-called M-20 Group—that's the December 20th National Liberation Group in longhand. They're a bunch of Noriega's cronies from the former Panamanian defense force, who regard the present government as treasonous and want to bring it down by force of arms. They set off bombs from time to time and run a death-squad operation that competes for victims with the other death squads, operated by the gang in power. The M-20 crowd goes after low-ranking officials now and then, while the main death squad mostly concentrates on common criminals and so-called left-wing dissidents."

"Sounds like a mess," the Executioner remarked.

"I wish that was the end of it."

"There's more?"

"They've got another liberation front of sorts, no name on this one, but it's working overtime to close down the drug routes and kick out the Triads. They don't mind striking at the other Chinese interests either, when they get a chance."

"Which side are we on?" Bolan asked.

"Officially, we're neutral," the big Fed replied. "But off the record, we would like to see the Triads blocked, at least. If something happened to the front men for the People's Army in the process, I've been told there won't be many tears in Washington."

"As long as it's deniable," Bolan amended.

"Well, of course. That's understood. We can't be seen to lift a hand against most-favored nations while we're pocketing their money, right?"

"This has a certain smell about it."

"I caught that, too," the man from Washington agreed. "I can't decide if it smells more like rotten fish or something that I stepped in once while I was visiting a dairy farm."

"But you're committed, right?"

"To have a look around," Brognola said. "No more, no less. You're free to pass, and no hard feelings. That's official."

"Let me have the rest of it."

"They've also got another no-name paramilitary outfit operating down there—a liberation army, call it what you want," Brognola said. "Not Reds, per se, as far as we can tell, but they don't care much for their present government officials."

"What's to like?" asked Bolan.

"Right. Good point," the man from Washington agreed. "Not much of anything, in fact. Communiqués from this group, though, aren't what you might expect from rebels in the area. There's nothing in the script about socialism, Marx or Lenin, Che Guevara, none of that. They don't have much to say about politics in general, when you get right down to it. Two things they can't abide are drug traffickers and your basic outside meddlers in the fate of Panama. That's more or less a quote," Brognola said, "and it includes us, right along with the Chinese and the Colombians."

"Sounds fair," the soldier remarked.

"To you and me, hell yes, but I can promise you it struck a sour note with certain folks at the State Department."

"I can imagine," Bolan said. "People who want to run their country by themselves. They must be stopped."

Brognola frowned. "It hasn't gotten that far yet," he said. "I'm hoping that it won't, but that's outside my bailiwick. I had some thoughts on how we might just head things off before it comes to that, however."

"What?"

"The leader of this no-name group—one of them, anyway—is a Guillermo Cruz. He's been involved in interdicting drug traffic from Colombia the past few months."

"Illegally?"

"Roger that," Brognola said. "The Triads and Colombian cartels are paid up on their graft, officially invisible. I wouldn't be surprised to learn they rate a military escort now and then, when things get rough."

"I take it things have gotten rough?"

"Seems like. The thing about Guillermo Cruz is that he doesn't like us much. No fan of Noriega, mind you, but he's read his history and takes it seriously. He'd prefer that all us gringos hit the road and let his people run their own affairs.''

''It doesn't sound like he'll be anxious to cooperate with anybody from the States,'' Bolan remarked.

''Well, there's a catch.''

''There always is. Let's hear it.''

''In a nutshell, when Guillermo and his buddies made up their minds to disrupt the flow of drugs through Panama, they weren't exactly clear on who the players were or how to go about it. So, of course, they had to get their pointers somewhere....''

''And they came to us,'' said Bolan, finishing the story for him.

''To the DEA, specifically. They've got a field office in Panama to keep tabs on all the traffic, but they can't do anything about it at the source. The way it works right now, they try to mark the shipments they can spot and have somebody waiting for the pickup when the product hits the States.''

''So, DEA's involved with this guerrilla outfit?'' Bolan asked. ''That doesn't sound like it would fit their brief.''

''You're right,'' Brognola said. ''It doesn't fit. They saw that right away, and Washington confirmed. Still, it was too damned sweet to throw away, you know? Somebody gave a heads-up to the CIA, and Langley's been coordinating, more or less. From what I understand, they've passed on a little surplus hardware, a little cash, some names and field surveillance information.''

''And the gang that doesn't like Americans becomes our client. Where have I heard that before?''

''It's vintage Langley,'' Brognola replied. ''Their standard operating procedure. From what I hear—and that's not much—they've had some problems with the operation, though. The Company was looking for some give-and-take, as usual, with emphasis on take. My guess would be they hoped to turn the locals into contract agents, but it hasn't worked, so far. Cruz and his buddies take the guns, the money and they make their hits, but any information they pass on is mostly drug related, shipments that they missed, like that.''

"So, Langley's in a snit," Bolan said.

Brognola responded with a shrug. "It could be worse," he said. "At least, if someone makes a stink about the Triads, somewhere down the road, the Company can say they did their best to root them out…within the rules, of course."

"Of course," Bolan replied. Deniability, again. The CIA had been restricted in its operations since the 1970s—at least, on paper. There were oversight committees on Capitol Hill, supposedly in touch with every operation mounted by American intelligence agencies, but no one in his right mind seriously believed the system was working, much less that it was foolproof. Covert activities would always be covert, and they would never end, as long as there were half a dozen people still alive on planet Earth scheming against their neighbors.

"Where do we fit in?" he asked his friend.

"Cruz and his people hit a major snag a few weeks back," Brognola said. "From what I get, they stopped another shipment, inbound from Colombia, but it turned out to be an ambush. There were extra shooters in the trucks and they had airborne military backup. Most of the guerrillas wound up getting waxed. Cruz got away somehow, but they've been hunting him."

"He should get out," said Bolan.

"That was the advice his contact gave him," the big Fed affirmed. "The guy's got a stubborn streak, I guess. Says 'he was born in Panama and plans to die there,' or words to that effect. My guess would be he'll get his wish before too long unless somebody helps him out."

"His crew's all gone?" asked Bolan.

"Not entirely, but they're spooked, with no morale to speak of. Langley has it worked out that they need a taste of victory to get their fighting spirit back, recruit new soldiers, start from scratch."

"Sounds reasonable," Bolan said. "Why isn't Langley taking care of it?"

"The truth? They're gun-shy. With the Red Chinese already digging in, and no complaints about it from the State Department, Langley figures either way they jump, they're screwed. If one of theirs gets caught in Panama, they'll hear about it from the Panamanians *and* the Chinese. Next thing you know, they'll have the White House and the oversight committees breathing down their necks while half the papers in the country run old stories on the Bay of Pigs. The Company's prepared to cut its losses, let the locals sink or swim."

"After they push them in the deep end of the pool," said Bolan.

"The Company rejects that inference, of course," Brognola remarked. "Officially, they had no part in any effort to disrupt commerce in Panama, legitimate or otherwise. If anybody asks, drug traffic is supposed to be controlled by DEA and Interpol. It's not a part of Langley's brief, and they would never overstep their bounds."

"If you can find somebody who believes that," Bolan said, "I have some beachfront property for sale in Arizona."

"Nobody *believes* it," Brognola replied. "It's smoke-and-mirrors time in Washington. The Company is innocent till proved guilty, and you'll never prove this case, because the files don't exist. As far as anybody knows, no one at Langley ever heard of a Guillermo Cruz, much less supplied him with illegal cash and weapons to promote guerrilla raids."

"Cruz still wants help, despite the fact that Langley's stabbed him in the back?" asked Bolan.

"Let's say he's not exactly current on the latest coffee chat from Washington," Brognola said. "He knows there's been a breakdown in communication, but his field contact is still in touch sporadically. He got approval to suggest that someone might be sent to help Cruz out, if they could swing it."

"And they came to you."

"Reluctantly. We're not exactly bosom pals," Brognola said, "but we still answer to The Man."

"You do," Bolan reminded him. "Not me."

"That's why I'm *asking* you," Hal said. "That's why you're free to take a pass, and no hard feelings."

Right. There might be no hard feelings on Brognola's part, but he would doubtless pay a price if Bolan turned down the mission. He could send Stony Man Farm's covert elite—Able Team or Phoenix Force—in Bolan's place, of course, but that meant risking several lives instead of one, and all of them were Bolan's friends. The flip side, meanwhile, was another negative. If no one went at all, Guillermo Cruz and his surviving allies would eventually be run to earth and killed. For what? For trying to prevent the spread of high-priced poison in their homeland and beyond.

"We need some ground rules," Bolan said.

"I'm listening."

"You said the locals have a contact from the Company."

"That's right," Brognola said. "Somebody from the embassy, I think."

"Okay. This contact gets the message through that someone's coming down to have a look around. No promises. He sets the meet, reports to you and then he's out of it. No contact whatsoever with Guillermo Cruz or anybody else, unless *I* get in touch with *him*. If I find out Langley's second-guessing me at any time, I'll mail their front man's head back to Virginia, on my way to the airport.''

''Done,'' the big Fed said. Bolan was sure his friend would phrase the ultimatum in more diplomatic language, but he didn't care. As long as Langley got the point and stayed out of his way, he would be satisfied.

''I'll need a charter or a military flight,'' the soldier continued. ''Something that will let me travel overweight without a penalty.'' He didn't have to spell it out, explain why he didn't want to travel naked, trusting weapons someone else had waiting for him at the other end.

''That's easy,'' said Brognola. ''I can get you on a military flight this afternoon.''

''Make it tomorrow,'' Bolan said. ''I have some things I need to do before I go.''

''Tomorrow it is.''

Bolan wasn't without misgivings as he thought about the trip to Panama, but nothing he had heard so far would put him off the mission. He would go and have a look around, meet with Guillermo Cruz and listen to the story from another angle. If the locals were amenable and if they could direct him to substantial targets, maybe back him up along the way, then Bolan would proceed. If anything smelled bad along the way or if it seemed to Bolan that the layout was a trap, he could withdraw.

Or so he hoped.

Some traps were cunningly concealed, and by the time you spotted them, they were already sprung. In that case, he would have to fight against whatever odds confronted him, as he had done in Southeast Asia in his lonely war against the Mafia, and in his long campaign against the predators identified by Hal Brognola and the team at Stony Man. He had survived this long by scoping out each situation as it came, and fighting like a demon when he had no other choice.

If it went sour on him in Panama, one thing was certain: anyone who thought the Executioner would be an easy mark was wrong. Dead wrong. No one who confronted him would walk away unscathed, and some of them, at least, would never walk away at all.

"You have the gear you'll need?"

"I'll check it out this afternoon," Bolan replied, "and requisition anything I'm missing."

"Fair enough," Brognola said. "Except for nukes or rolling stock, the Farm should have most anything you'd want. Or I could pull some other strings."

"I'll let you know."

Bolan wasn't a pessimist, though some would doubtless label him a fatalist. He didn't plan on carting tons of martial hardware down to Panama, but he would be prepared. That meant sufficient weaponry to let him deal with varied situations as they came, responding on the basis of experience and expertise. A decent sniper's rifle, certain automatic weapons, side arms, ample ammunition for the lot, a useful mix of plastique and grenades.

In short, the usual.

"If anything about this strikes you funny once you're down there," Brognola was saying, "pull the pin and come back home, ASAP. I don't like cleaning up for Langley, as it is. I wouldn't want to lose you on some frigging snipe hunt."

"Not to worry," Bolan told his friend. "One thing I know is when to quit."

Brognola laughed aloud at that. "Oh, sure," he said, when he could find his voice again. "You know, all right, but doing it's another ball game, right? I mean this, Striker. The first sign of a double cross, you hightail out of there and don't think twice about it. Any funny business from the Company, we'll sort it out and figure what the spooks have coming for their trouble. And I guarantee you, payback is a bitch.''

''You have some reason to suspect they're stringing you along?'' Bolan asked.

''No,'' Brognola grudgingly admitted. ''But they specialize in playing both ends off against the middle. You know that as well as anyone.''

He did, indeed. A traitor in the CIA had cost Bolan the second great love of his life and threatened the very existence of Stony Man Farm, once upon a time, and the traitor had paid with his life. The Company itself hadn't been privy to the actions of a rogue force in the ranks, but Langley's own official history was rife with double-dealing, rank betrayal, sudden shifts in policy that left loyal allies stranded on the killing fields. It would be nothing new for Covert Ops to play some hidden angle, calculate the sacrifice required to gain some secret payoff, and to hell with anyone who fell along the way. Bolan took that for granted, going in and he wasn't about to leave his back unprotected around anyone who served the Company.

As for Guillermo Cruz and his resistance fighters, any bond they forged with Bolan would be tenuous at best. Suspicious of outsiders and especially of Americans, they might be reticent to deal with him at all, much less invest him with the trust that was required of men in mortal combat.

All that remained for Bolan to sort out once he was on the ground in Panama. For now, he had the raw mechanics of his job to focus on: logistics and material, the mental preparation that a mission out of country normally required.

''I'd better get back to the office,'' Brognola remarked.

''No problem,'' Bolan said. ''I'll be in touch.''

He watched his friend walk away, retreating through tidy rows of grave markers, stepping over heroes as he went. It struck him that the crowded soil of Arlington, for all the fighting men and women buried there, was no more than a thumbnail sketch of sacrifice. For every hero represented there, how many thousands more were buried elsewhere? How many were lost beyond recall—at sea, in foreign jungles—vaporized by shellfire and explosives?

Bolan had no great, compelling urge to join them, but he understood their motivations. Some had fought for God and country, others for their units or their buddies on the firing line. Some had expected death, while others had been taken by surprise.

But all of them had done their duty, seen it through and paid the final price. There was a lesson in their sacrifice, and he could do no less.

"I'll see you later," Bolan told the silent dead, and started on the walk back to his car.

3

"You know my name?" Guillermo Cruz was startled, even after all that had transpired within the past few moments, corpses scattered in the street, with fresh blood glinting crimson in the sunlight. With the gunfire's echoes still ringing in his ears, the sound of his own name, pronounced by unfamiliar lips, made him clutch the Walther that much tighter.

"We had a date at the Café Europa." As the stranger spoke, Cruz saw him wave his left hand, the one with the larger of his pistols, vaguely toward the men whom he had slain. "We really ought to talk about this somewhere else."

"These men…"

"Are dead," the gringo said. "And if I'm not mistaken, they had something very similar in mind for you. I'm leaving now. Unless you want to hang around and talk to the security police you should consider joining me."

Cruz kept the Walther in his hand, though something told him it would do no good against this man who killed as easily as others wiped sweat from their brow. Perhaps it was machismo, but the pistol made Cruz feel as if he had some measure of control over what happened next, all logic to the contrary.

He walked around the gringo's car and got in on the passenger side, holding the Walther in his lap. He didn't use the seat belt, just in case he felt a sudden urge to bolt and fling himself out of the car. It was ridiculous, of course—the man had saved his life, for Mary's sake!—but paranoia had become a way of life for Cruz and his surviving coterie of friends in Panama.

"My name's Belasko," said the stranger, as the car turned at the intersection, leaving death behind them. "Mike Belasko. I was asked to speak with you and see if maybe I could help you out, short term."

"You're from the CIA?" Cruz asked. He was embarrassed by the tremor in his voice, amazed that lethal violence still had this effect on him, in spite of all he'd seen and done. Was that humanity at work, or simple weakness?

Belasko made another turn before he said, "Not CIA. We keep in touch, from time to time, but I don't work for them."

"Who, then?"

"You might say I'm an independent troubleshooter."

Cruz picked out the sounds of distant sirens, growing closer by the moment, but the gringo didn't seem concerned.

"I think we'd better skip the restaurant," was all he said. "They'll be looking for you. Is there somewhere we can go to talk?"

It struck Guillermo Cruz that he was homeless, once again. His true home, in the northern suburbs of the city, had been burned by unknown "patriots" the year before when he began to speak out publicly against the drug trade and the growing Chinese influence in Panama. Police had milled around the scene, poked through the smoking rubble of his life and told him that they would investigate. Cruz saw them smirking as they left and he wasn't surprised when no one ever called him back.

It could have been much worse, he realized, if he had been a married man with children in the house. A few weeks later, when he lost his teaching job, dismissed for "inefficiency," Cruz knew that the corrupt regime would never let him rest until he fled his homeland or was buried there. It still took him another month to join the small but growing rebel underground, and he had risen quickly through the ranks once he had proved himself in action. In a movement made up of recruits who were mostly laborers and peasants, Cruz had became the intellectual in residence, a strategist and spokesman for the cause.

And he had led his comrades to disaster in the mountains—and watched them die.

Since then, the closest thing he knew to "home" had been a string of roach-infested flats, with common toilets shared by upward of two dozen tenants. He couldn't go back to the apartment where the snatch team had been waiting for him, and he ran a mental checklist of the items he had lost: some clothes, a second pair of shoes, his razor, toothbrush, half a dozen books, some extra ammunition for the Walther.

Nothing that he couldn't live without.

But, where to take Mike Belasko now?

He knew the answer instantly, but hesitated, nonetheless. It was a firm, unwritten rule that one didn't place comrades needlessly at risk. This comrade in particular was special, valued by Guillermo Cruz for reasons that were only half political. Still, there was no denying what the gringo said. Whether the men who had tried to take him on the sidewalk were police or unofficial killers from the death squad, Cruz had no doubt whatsoever that he would be charged with killing them. Four counts of murder with a note that he was armed and dangerous would give the state security police a license to shoot him on sight.

"There is a place," he said at last, reluctantly, "but I must telephone first."

Belasko glanced at him—was that suspicion in the gringo's eyes?—and shrugged before he said, "Okay. Let's find a phone."

They drove for several blocks before Cruz spied a petrol station on the left, a pay phone mounted on the wall beside the entrance to the rest room. "There," he said pointing, before slouching lower in his seat as Belasko pulled into the station and around the side to park close by the telephone.

Cruz knew that he was paranoid when he imagined the attendant, in his denim coveralls, was staring at him while he wiped the windshield of a Ford sedan. Cruz tucked the Walther in the waistband of his slacks, well hidden by his jacket, and was careful not to let it show as he exited the car. Coins jingled in his pocket, and his palm was sweaty as he sorted through them, dropping two into the telephone before he dialed.

A cautious voice responded on the second ring. "*Sí?*"

He was tempted to cradle the receiver but he glanced back at the car and found his gringo savior watching him. Cruz swallowed hard and said, "It's me."

"JUST UP AHEAD," Cruz told him. "Pull into the alley, there."

Despite the confident directions, Bolan took his time. He didn't think Guillermo Cruz would double-cross him, most particularly not while Cruz was in the line of fire himself, but caution was a way of life for Bolan. It had kept him breathing through repeated clashes where he found himself outnumbered and outgunned. Part of the trick was confidence, but that could only take a fighting man so far. You could be confident and dead, if you forgot to watch your back.

"Park anywhere along this side," Cruz said. "It's permitted for the residents."

"Police don't check?" asked Bolan, as he nosed into a spot behind a ten-year-old Toyota.

"In this neighborhood," his guide replied sardonically,

"police come only if there are reports of workers' protests or a killing. If it's merely homicide, they take their time. These folk don't really matter, after all."

Cruz made no effort to conceal his bitterness. Bolan locked the car and trailed his escort through a gate into the courtyard of an old apartment complex. He kept one hand at his waist, thumb hooked inside his belt, prepared to go for the Beretta 93-R on a heartbeat's notice. If a trap was waiting for him, it would spring somewhere between the gate and the apartment they were seeking.

Cruz led Bolan up a flight of rusty metal stairs, along a balcony of sorts that overlooked the courtyard. Below, some spiky yucca plants had gone to seed in what was once a cactus garden, surviving in rugged defiance of abject neglect. Apartment doors along the tier were painted brown, some of them faded, others freshly done, with signs of patchwork mending where they had been broken and repaired.

Cruz stopped before one of the doors and glanced back at Bolan before he knocked. Though he used relatively little force, the whole door seemed to rattle in its frame, a sign of cheap construction and advancing age. Some moments passed before they heard a bolt and chain released inside, the door swinging open to admit them without revealing a soul.

Bolan had his hand on the Beretta as he entered, sidestepping to clip the open door with his elbow, forcing it wider, crowding anyone who might have tried to hide behind it. As it turned out, there was no ambush, just a stunningly attractive woman standing off to Bolan's left, the short-barreled revolver in her right hand pointed at the floor.

She didn't try to raise the weapon as Cruz closed the door and double locked it. Bolan eased his hand away from the Beretta, calculating that it would be no great trick to close the gap between them and disarm her, even break her neck if necessary, should she try to aim and fire. She regarded him with caution, not fear.

Guillermo Cruz stepped between them and performed the introductions. "Mike Belasko, this is Ariana. Ariana, Mike Belasko, from *El Norte*."

She made no move to offer him her hand, holding the snubby .38 revolver down against her thigh. "You're from the CIA?" she asked.

He shook his head and nodded toward Guillermo Cruz. "No, we've already covered that, Ms....?"

"Vasquez," she finished for him. "You may call me Ariana, as Guillermo said."

He glanced around the small apartment. A waist-high counter separated a tiny kitchen from the living room, with one stool offering a place to sit while dining. Off to Bolan's left, beyond the woman, two doors standing open offered him a glimpse of a bedroom and a claustrophobically sized bathroom. Bolan judged they were alone, although he didn't let down his guard.

Not yet.

"Sit, please," Vasquez said. As she gestured toward a couch and two overstuffed chairs in the living room, she caught herself raising the pistol to point and blushed as she turned to place it on the kitchen countertop. "Something to drink, perhaps? Iced tea? Beer?"

Bolan waited for Cruz to respond. He asked for beer, and the soldier took a chance on the iced tea. There was a possibility it might be drugged or poisoned but he didn't think so. Vasquez's blush had done the trick for him, as much as anything. The lady might hang out with rebels, might even be one herself, but she didn't strike Bolan as a cold-blooded conspirator. In any case, if they were going to cooperate, however briefly, they would have to trust each other within certain limits, and it may as well begin with him.

He took one of the chairs, while Cruz sat on the couch. When Vasquez brought the drinks, she settled in the other easy chair forming a triangle of sorts. Cruz seemed to frown when she didn't sit beside him on the couch. Was it imagination, or did Cruz harbor an interest in the lady of the house beyond their common political cause? Bolan wasn't concerned about their personal relationship, or lack of the same, unless it somehow managed to become a stumbling block. If Cruz allowed himself to be distracted by romance or jealousy, then it would be a problem. Otherwise...

The tea was sweet, and Bolan smiled approval at their hostess. "I suppose the easy way is just to tell you what I know, and let you fill in any blanks," he said, "if that's all right with you."

Cruz sipped his beer straight from the bottle, nodding as he swallowed. "Yes, by all means. Please proceed."

He ran it down from scratch, omitting any mention of Brognola or specific links to any U.S. agency: the Triads and the Red Chinese in Panama, the drug trade, the Panama Harbor Authority, attempts by Cruz and company to interdict the narco traffic. When he finished, both of them were watching him, exchanging sidelong glances. Vasquez seeming more relaxed, while Cruz still wore what seemed to be his customary frown.

"So far, so good?" the Executioner inquired.

"You're correct in what you say," Cruz told him. Vasquez watched him without speaking, sipping her iced tea. Her snub-nosed .38 revolver seemed to be forgotten on the dining counter.

"All right then," Bolan said. "So, what I need from you would be specific names, locations, anything at all to help me check out the problem and see if something can be done."

"Something will certainly be done," Guillermo Cruz replied. "The only question is when, and by whom."

"Okay take your time and fill me in." That said, Bolan settled back into his chair to wait.

"Perhaps," Cruz said by way of introduction, "you would like to meet some of our comrades in this war we fight?"

MAJOR MIGUEL DUENDE loved his job. If called upon to do so, he could even count the ways he loved it, like that silly gringo poem he had read sometime, somewhere.

One reason Major Duende loved his job was that it made him wealthy. Not as rich as the president or certain other statesmen, but his bank accounts were fat and his home was luxurious beyond the wildest dreams of dwellers in the peasant village he had fled, to wear a uniform when he was seventeen years old.

That uniform itself was yet another reason why Duende loved his job. Now that he had a decent rank, gold braid, some shiny medals, women melted at the very sight of him. He charmed them with his wit and stories of his courage under fire. They finished melting when they saw what he was packing *underneath* the uniform, and begged for him to take them, fill them, use them any way he liked. On rare occasions when he found a woman who wasn't impressed by men in uniform, he found another way to break her down, and she would beg him just the same.

And that was what Duende loved about his life's work most of all: the power. As commander of the state security police, Duende literally held the power over life and death for those who fell into his hands. In the decade since the Yankees came for Noriega, they had numbered in the thousands, mostly peasants like his own forebears, but with a sprinkling of snotty college students and decadent aging rebels for variety. Duende broke them all, deciding in the process who could serve him in exchange for mercy, who would live and who would die.

So many dead, and yet it still infuriated him to hear that one had managed to escape.

"You idiot!" he raged. "Four men? This peasant you were told to deal with killed four men and got away?"

Adolfo Quintana swallowed the abuse and let it go. He was too wise to challenge Duende. As leader of the largest paramilitary death squad in the district, he was used to walking on the razor's edge between official sanction and a shallow grave.

"The pig had help, *Jefé*," Quintana said. "Two different guns were used against my men. A witness says she saw two men drive off."

"A witness in *that* neighborhood?" Duende sneered. "And you believe her?"

"She was most emphatic. As were the interrogators."

"Very well. Two men against your four, with your men holding the advantage of surprise. That's very disappointing. Shoddy work. You should have killed them both."

"There's one thing more," Quintana said.

"By all means, let us have more thrilling news, Adolfo."

"One of them, the second man…he was a gringo."

"The woman said this?" Duende asked, his mocking tone subdued for once, though he couldn't have said exactly why.

"*Sí, Jefé.*"

"She couldn't have been mistaken?" Duende challenged.

"She believed what she was saying, this I know," Quintana said. "Of course, that doesn't mean she is correct."

"Of course," the major said. He should have felt relieved, with logic kicking in, but somehow he wasn't convinced by his own rationalization.

Duende spent a moment staring at the large map on his

office wall, bright-colored pins marking dozens of locations: blue pins for rural villages judged loyal to the state;
red for those sympathetic to—or controlled by—rebel
forces; black for villages that had been sanitized by force.

What did it matter if a gringo had arrived to help Guillermo Cruz? Perhaps nothing. Or, then again, perhaps a
great deal. It would depend on who the gringo was, and
more importantly, who sent him. Those were questions that
Guillermo Cruz might answer, but Duende much preferred
to hear their answers from the nameless gringo himself. If
there was such a man.

"I want them both," he told Quintana, speaking clearly
so that there could be no claim of a misunderstanding later.
"I want both of them alive and fit to talk. Do what you
must, disable them if necessary, but I shall expect to hear
their voices with my own two ears. And I expect to hear
them soon. You understand, Adolfo?"

"*Sí, Jefé.*" Quintana frowned. "If Cruz had called on
friends in the United States—"

"Then we will deal with them," Duende cut him off.
"Go do your job, now. Let me tend to mine."

Quintana left without another word, without a backward
glance. If he was angry, so much the better, Duende
thought. Let his rage provide him with the energy that he
would need to track his quarry and to bring them back
alive.

Major Duende, meanwhile, had more pressing matters on
his mind. He had prepared another strike against the rebels
for that very afternoon. If nothing went amiss, by nightfall
he would have eradicated one more nest of treason, and
perhaps the worst of them, at that. Duende knew the rebel
forces had been whittled down through combat losses, mass
arrests and defections. There would always be some stupid
peasants standing by to take the place of those who fell or

went to prison, but the number of replacements had been dwindling in the face of his relentless persecution.

Why not use the dreaded word? Major Duende persecuted those who threatened Panama, and did so gladly, sleeping well at night. More to the point, he also hounded, persecuted and annihilated those who threatened him. The life-style he had come to treasure since the fall of Noriega gave him room to breathe and to expand his own authority.

This day, if all went well, he would deliver one more crushing blow to those who schemed against him, sought to bring him down and leave him mired in poverty, perhaps locked in a prison cell or worse. If those he sent to do the job were swift and ruthless enough, the threat might be crushed, Guillermo Cruz reduced to just another crank who could be dealt with at Duende's leisure.

There was still the gringo to be hunted down, of course, but he would let Quintana deal with that problem...at least, for now.

Duende reached toward the map, removed one of the crimson pins and placed it in a metal tray that ran the full width of the map, much like the chalk tray on the blackboard in his childhood school. He found a black pin, smiling as he picked it up and placed it in the red pin's place, same hole, working with surgical precision.

There, Major Duende thought. Take that. And burn in hell.

COLONEL BAO BAI-FAN ignored the telephone, leaving one of his aides to hoist the receiver and see who was pleading for extra attention this time. The colonel was a firm believer in delegating authority, especially when it came to off-loading the petty annoyances of daily life. Why have subordinates at all if they weren't assigned the lion's share of drudgery and dirty work?

Colonel Bao was no stranger to the realm of dirty work,

of course. He had come up through the ranks of the People's Army, starting as a private in the early 1970s, advancing by virtue of obedience, cunning and raw intelligence until he reached his present rank. The colonel's hands were far from clean, but he had always seen his duty through without complaint. Whether that duty took him into Burma or Cambodia, Africa or Canada, he got the job done and was suitably rewarded for his efforts over time.

Passing the full-length mirror in his den, Bao still experienced a moment of surprise when he glimpsed himself in the custom-tailored business suit. It was a far cry from the military uniform in which he felt at home, but the reaction still disturbed him. He had worked so often undercover that he should be used to it by now, instead of feeling like a turtle who had somehow lost his shell and found himself exposed to countless enemies.

Bao had no doubt regarding the nature of his job in Panama. The climate was no worse than Burma—or Myanmar, as the peasants called it now—but he despised the people he was forced to deal with in the execution of his duties. Execution. There had been a time, not long ago, when the colonel would cheerfully have executed those who were now his grudging allies: the Triad bastards with their drugs and sneering ridicule of socialism, their contempt for law itself. How many of them had he ordered shot for smuggling opium and heroin in better days? Now, here he was, assigned to work with those he should have hunted down like rats, but compelled by orders from Beijing to help facilitate their traffic in narcotics.

All because of the canal.

Bao understood the opportunity his nation and the People's Struggle had encountered in Panama. Effective military leaders understood geography as well as weapons, tactics and troop deployment. Anyone with half a brain could recognize how critical the Panama Canal might be, strategically, in the new century. Why else had Beijing and the People's Army invested so much in the Panama Harbor Authority, installing banker Lin Shao-pei as their front man of record? Why else was Colonel Bao attached to the Chinese embassy in Panama City, masquerading as a cultural attaché and coordinating payoffs to the local government, cooperating with the hated Triad gangsters?

Bao heard his aide approaching, turned to face the younger man and waited to be told which VIP demanded precious moments of his time. His passive face betrayed no irritation. Colonel Bao had learned to keep his feelings locked away inside, his lips sealed tightly against intemperate remarks.

"Major Duende, sir," his aide declared, "from the security police."

As if there could be two Major Duendes in the world, Bao thought, resisting the impulse to sneer. While he was trained in use of force and had applied it frequently in China and in outposts of the revolution circling the globe, Bao still reserved a fine contempt for petty Third World despots who enriched themselves at gunpoint, preying on their own. If it had been his choice, Bao would have placed Duende up against the wall beside his good friends from the Triad and shot them all without a second thought. But sometimes local tyrants had their uses.

It wouldn't be feasible for Chinese troops to enter Panama in force. Bao understood the need for subterfuge, establishment of paper companies, cooperation with the locals and the scum who dealt in poison, but he didn't have to like it. He would do his duty, as he always had, and hope the rancid smell washed off when he was done.

Lifting the telephone receiver on his desk, the colonel feigned a tone of pleasure as he spoke. "Major Duende, greetings. May I be of some assistance?"

"No, señor," the major said in English, forgetting once

again that Colonel Bao was fluent in Spanish and four other languages. "I simply called to say that I'm hoping to resolve our problem with the rebel scum this afternoon."

Bao frowned, recalling that Duende had been predicting victory for months on end. Each time he struck against the peasants who bedeviled them, the major claimed to think his latest stroke would be the last required. Bao wondered, not for the first time, if Duende was a pathological liar or simply incompetent, but he would no more voice that question aloud than he would spit in the face of his nation's premier.

Instead, he told the pig, "That is most welcome news, comrade. I wish your soldiers great success." That much was true, at least. Bao hoped the major's men would finally destroy the peasant outlaws who should rightfully have been suppressed three months before when they began attacking Triad shipments from Colombia.

"We don't need luck, Señor," Duende told him, arrogant despite the string of failures that had marked his efforts to eliminate the rebels. Duende's men had managed to run up a body count, of course—assisted by the unofficial death squads, yet another feature of the region Bao would never fully understand—but each new slaughter only seemed to spark an armed reaction from the enemy. Instead of losing heart, the rebels learned from their mistakes and rededicated themselves to the extermination of their enemies in power.

Bao was reminded of his grade-school studies, the lesson of Chairman Mao and the Long March to victory over Chiang Kai-shek. His teachers had presented the lesson because it was required by law, a critical indoctrination feature for upcoming generations in the People's Republic, but there was another lesson to be learned from the Long March, as well.

If rebel movements weren't crushed decisively, and early

on, they would inevitably spread and triumph in the end. Each time Duende missed the leaders of the movement and allowed surviving remnants of their peasant army to regroup, he made another deadly error. Bao wasn't empowered to correct him, dared not even hint at the inadequacy of his native counterpart, but he could see it all the same. And he was worried more and more, that any failure on Duende's part would somehow blacken *his* good name, when word of the disaster reached Beijing.

Bao thought it might be time to intercede, though he would have to do so cautiously, discreetly, bearing the delicate feelings and mercurial tempers of the natives constantly in mind. Perhaps, he thought, there was a way to let the Triads do it, and to thus assume the risk of any failure for themselves.

"Thank you for calling, Major." Colonel Bao was almost smiling now, the plan already taking shape behind his cold gray eyes. "I shall look forward to reports of your success."

4

The road trip was an unexpected twist. Bolan had planned on talking to Guillermo Cruz, securing the information he required then making up his mind about participating in the game. He had already played one round and scored four points against the enemy, but there was still a chance for him to disengage and let the locals fight it out among themselves before he was identified as a participant.

The road trip changed all that. Cruz had wanted him to meet the other rebels—those that still remained, after six weeks of pounding from the state security police and paramilitary death squads. They had gathered in some kind of mountain camp, roughly a hundred miles southwest of Panama City. When Bolan met them, Cruz told him, then he would understand their struggle, realize why they couldn't surrender or simply slip away.

Bolan had thought about dismissing the request, but then decided he would ride along. It must have been imagination, he supposed that made him think the woman—Ariana Vasquez—had been pleased by his decision. It wasn't imagination, though, when she announced her plan to tag along.

"The city isn't safe, Guillermo," she replied, as Cruz was starting to object. "Would you have those who tried to take you come for me?"

Cruz caved on that one, and the woman flashed a smile at Bolan, looking satisfied. "Why don't we take my car?"

Bolan suggested, thinking of the hardware he was carrying which he didn't care to leave behind, unguarded.

"It has four-wheel drive?" Cruz asked him.

Bolan shook his head. "I wasn't planning on an off-road rally," he replied.

"We need the four-wheel for the last part of our journey," Cruz explained, "and even then, there comes a time when we must walk. Security, you understand? But, never mind. I have a vehicle that we can use."

"I'll need to bring some bags along," said Bolan. "From my car."

Cruz frowned at that, but wasted no time arguing. "Bring what you like," he said, "as long as we can fit it in the jeep."

"Sounds fair."

The jeep in question was an ancient ragtop, plastic windows on the sides and rear as cloudy and stained as a chain-smoker's lungs. Bolan had no idea how old the jeep was, but he wouldn't have been shocked to learn that it had gone ashore on Iwo Jima, maybe Omaha Beach.

He sat in back with his bags and a ten-gallon fuel can, letting Ariana Vasquez take the shotgun seat, with Cruz behind the wheel. Bolan had thought the young man might want to inspect his luggage, but the rebel made no move in that direction—though he cocked an eyebrow when the larger bag produced a clanking sound on contact with the metal floorboard of the jeep.

"You don't travel light, Belasko," Cruz remarked.

"Old Boy Scout," Bolan told him. "Be prepared."

That won a laugh from Vasquez as they started on their way. Cruz wore a pair of dated wraparound shades and he had changed his clothes, discarding the suit in favor of casual denim, topping it off with an old Yankees cap. It wasn't much of a disguise for someone who was being hunted by the state police and hired-gun vigilantes, but then again Cruz didn't strike Bolan as much of an actor. The lump beneath his loose shirt, on the right, would be some kind of side arm wedged into his belt, and Bolan wondered if the guy was any good with it.

Their pretty shotgun rider hadn't changed her clothes, except to put on well-worn hiking shoes. Plastic shades were the extend of her disguise. Bolan had no idea if she was wanted by the state, if anyone outside the rebel camp knew who she was or recognized her link to the guerrillas, and he didn't let it bother him. He wanted to trust both of these new people who were passing briefly through his life, but that required some time. While he was working up to it, it only made good sense to let them sit up front where neither one of them could casually put a pistol to his head or slip a noose around his neck.

Constant suspicion was a fact of life in Bolan's world and had been from the relatively early days when he was hunted by the Mafia on two continents. He didn't jump at shadows, but he always checked them out to make sure nothing dangerous was hiding in the dark. And when his work for Hal Brognola took him to a foreign country locked in turmoil, where the players were confused and frequently duplicitous, he never let his guard down all the way. An enemy who caught him in the shower, on the toilet, even making love, would still find it a challenge to surprise the Executioner.

Between the powerful Beretta 93R in its shoulder rig and the assorted hardware resting at his feet, Bolan felt reasonably confident that he could deal with any trap that might be waiting for him in the mountains. He didn't believe that Cruz would plan an ambush of the vehicle with Vasquez seated only inches to his right. If there was treachery afoot it would be waiting for him at the camp, but Bolan's gut was urging him to trust these two. And their compatriots? Well, he would simply have to wait and see.

They followed the Pan-American Highway for the first hour of their journey, leaving Panama City behind. A few miles past San Carlos, Cruz slowed and started searching for a side road that was both unlabeled and, as Bolan soon found out, unpaved. Five minutes more and they had lost sight of the highway, bumping over ruts and potholes, Bolan braced himself with one hand while planting a foot on each of his bags to keep them from jostling. He wished the jeep had seat belts in the back, but judged that they weren't going fast enough for any accident to do much human damage.

Out of nowhere, a recruiting slogan flashed through his mind; one of those cooked up by the U.S. military when the draft had been abolished in the early 1970s: It's not just a job; it's an adventure.

Right.

And as their track grew steeper by the moment, Bolan watched the forest crowding them, determined that this adventure wouldn't be his last.

CAPTAIN LUIS PEREZ was chosen for the airborne raid because his troops had done so well their last time out. As he had hoped, the men who cut his orders were impressed, though they weren't demonstrative or lavish in their praise. Such things were rarely mentioned, but Perez knew they were written down somewhere, and would be scanned with interest when his next shot at promotion came. What more could he expect?

This time, instead of two Blackhawks, he had been given three, with forty soldiers under his command. It was an honor, but it also made the captain nervous, since he knew only a handful of the soldiers and couldn't be certain how they would react in combat, whether they would follow his commands or panic under fire.

As in the last airborne attack, he hoped it wouldn't matter. Each Blackhawk was fully armed with .50-caliber Gatling guns and four rocket pods each, for a grand total of 304 high-explosive 70 mm rockets. With that much firepower, and at least some measure of surprise, Captain Perez knew he could wipe a fair-sized army off the map.

He had been told his target was a camp or village in the mountains where the rebels went to hide. It was supposed to harbor only soldiers, but Perez wasn't concerned about the possibility of noncombatants getting in his way. He understood that those who gave the rebels aid and comfort were as dangerous—perhaps more so, in fact—than those who carried arms and fought. If they were women, that meant that they were breeders of rebellion, sources of contagion handed down through peasant generations in the blood. As for the children, they would only grow to hate his kind and wage a new guerrilla war someday...if they grew up at all. The gringos had a motto for such situations, often silk-screened onto T-shirts: Kill Them All, And Let God Sort Them Out.

Why not?

It was a brutal, bloody business, but which war wasn't? Who could expect to walk a battlefield and come back home again without some bloodstains on his boots? The end did justify the means, when everything Perez had known and trusted from his childhood was in jeopardy. He didn't care to think about the rebels, what their side was fighting for. It was enough to know that they opposed him, wished him dead, and further sought to undermine the very state he served. The state that paid his wages, put clothes on his children's backs. What more was there to know?

Their strike was timed to coincide with the siesta hour, someone in authority presuming that guerrillas hiding in the mountains followed the same schedule as shopkeepers in town. For all the captain knew, it might be so. He meant to see his orders carried out in any case and hoped their argets might be taken by surprise, perhaps while dining, maybe dozing in the shade. There would be no disguising heir approach, of course, but speed and firepower would surely compensate for that.

Of late, Captain Perez had come to relish fighting from he air, though he hadn't been trained specifically in such procedures. He had spent the early part of his career pursuing bandits and subversives on the ground, which meant interminable marches through the steaming jungle, terrified—though he dared not admit it—that an ambush might be waiting for him when he took his next step. Airborne assault removed those fears, once Perez had overcome his even greater fear of plummeting to earth—the Blackhawks were, in Yankee parlance, eminently crashworthy. He quickly came to realize that flying into battle gave great advantages: supreme firepower, three-dimensional mobility, capacity for zooming out of small-arms range at a moment's notice, and the classic bird's-eye view, which left his targets scrambling below like insects with nowhere to hide. Captain Perez enjoyed that feeling. Sometimes, it was better than sex.

While not a coward, neither was the captain careless with his life, as were some officers and soldiers he had known. Perez wasn't a suicidal glory hound. His quest for recognition and advancement in the military was inevitably tempered by the knowledge that a corpse derives no satisfaction from awards and praise. He didn't crave a hero's funeral. He preferred to bury those he was assigned to track and kill.

Today's assault, he understood, would be a major victory against the rebel forces, if he didn't let too many of them slip away. Determined not to fail, he scanned the troops seated before him in the Blackhawk, each man with an M-16 assault rifle clasped between his knees. They looked so young, Perez was moved to speculate that this might be

the first taste of combat for some. It should be relativel
easy, once the rebel camp had been reduced by rocket fir
and strafing runs, but he would watch them closely, just i
case. And woe be to any man who showed a hint of weak
ness on the firing line.

Perez checked his wristwatch, estimating that they ha
another twenty minutes left to wait before they reached th
target zone. He felt the old, familiar flutter in his stomacl
that preceded any violent action in the field. Perez coul
only hope his men wouldn't disgrace themselves and tha
he would survive the coming fight intact.

They were over the mountains and climbing, fighting a
updraft, and he made a show of glancing at his watch again
not really seeing it. His men looked restless, and he wante
them to think he was relaxed, despite the Blackhawk'
bucking in midair. Crashworthy it might be, but he coul
not afford to think about the densely wooded peaks a thou
sand feet below them. No one could survive that kind o
fall, seat belts or not.

Captain Perez surveyed his men once more and foun
some of them watching him. He made eye contact, but h
wouldn't smile. There was no place for such familiarit
between an officer and his enlisted men. It was enough fo
him to demonstrate that he wasn't afraid. And if they swal
lowed that, Perez thought he deserved a nomination for th
gringo Academy Awards. Best Actor of the year for a per
formance in a lurching, reeling helicopter.

His stomach had begun to churn, and Perez was worrie
that he might disgrace himself by vomiting when suddenl
the turbulence was gone. One moment, they were rockin
in their seats, unwilling passengers on a wild carnival ride
while the next they were cruising dead level and perfectl
calm. Captain Perez allowed his pent-up breath to exhale
through his nostrils slowly, counting on the helicopter'
engine noise to cover any sounds of his relief.

Next stop, the killing fields.

Another quick glance at his wrist, immediately followed by a curt announcement from the pilot telling everyone aboard that they were closing on their target.

"Weapons check!" Perez commanded. He listened to the sound of thirteen rifle bolts as they were thrown to chamber armor-piercing rounds. "Remember, when we hit the ground," he said, "no prisoners!"

ENRIQUE ESPINOSA was on sentry duty when the helicopters came in from the east, skimming at treetop level. Crewmen stood in the open bays behind their Gatling guns. He should have heard them sooner but he was distracted, crouching in the ferns with baggy pants around his ankles, straining to relieve himself.

Something he ate, of course—Enrique's biggest problem was that he ate anything and everything in sight—and now it seemed he was about to die for it.

The helicopters circled once around the clearing where the camp had been established under nets of tattered camouflage before the gunners opened fire. Enrique Espinosa wondered, as he grappled with his pants and dropped his M-1 carbine, how the raiders found them.

It hardly mattered now. The nets were coming down as streams of automatic fire descended from the circling helicopters, slashing the support lines, ripping into tents and shanties, chewing up the forest floor. Espinosa heard men cursing and women screaming as the bullets found them. He could smell the stench of cordite wafting down from overhead.

The sudden racket had unleashed a storm of fruit bats from the trees around him, startled from their daytime sleep, swooping and screeching as they fled the slaughter zone. Espinosa ducked and threw an arm across his face as they swarmed past him, recoiling from the touch of their tenebrous wings. When they were gone he finished grappling with his belt and stooped to fetch his carbine, cocking it before he turned to face the carnage in the camp.

What could he do to help? Espinosa knew the helicopters used by military troops were armored to resist small-arms fire, but could still be brought to earth if lucky bullets found the engines, rotor blades or pilots. Espinosa wasn't sure if he could do such damage with his carbine but he knew he had to try. Already, his neglect of duty had betrayed his comrades, costing precious lives and he must act without delay in order to redeem himself.

Espinosa had been positioned on the west side of the camp, while the attackers had approached from the northeast. He wondered what had happened to the other sentries, but he had no time to study the problem or go looking for the other posted guards. He had covered half the hundred-meter distance from his post to the encampment, rushing headlong through the forest with his carbine held in front of him to clear the way of dangling fronds and branches. He believed there still might be a chance for him to help…but then all holy hell broke loose.

At first, Espinosa thought a tracer round from one of the machine guns must have found a fuel can near the mess tent or perhaps drilled one of half a dozen motorcycles parked beneath the camo netting. The explosion stopped him in his tracks and nearly knocked him over with a gust of superheated wind, but Espinosa knew he was mistaken when he heard another detonation and another, coming one behind the other like a string of giant firecrackers.

It took a moment for his throbbing ears to recognize the swoosh of rockets flying from the helicopter gunships, streaking earthward to explode in roiling smoke and flame. One of those rockets found the mess tent causing the fuel cans to explode, a fiery secondary blast that spattered running men with petrol, setting them ablaze.

"Madre de díos!"

It was like a scene from Hell, as Espinosa's village priest had once described it to him when he was a child. The only difference, he realized, was that the torment of these dying souls wouldn't be everlasting. They were dropping right before his eyes, some smoldering in crumpled heaps of blackened flesh, while others twitched and danced to the erratic tune of the machine guns. Two children ran across his field of vision, screaming, then were chopped down in their tracks by automatic fire. Espinosa felt his last meal coming back, erupting from his stomach in a sour rush of bile.

"You bastards!"

Torn between an urge to flee and sudden, bitter hatred he had never known before, Enrique Espinosa stood his ground for six or seven seconds more, then made his choice, continuing in the direction of the camp that had become a slaughterhouse. It was a hopeless task, he realized—the next best thing to suicide—but still, he had to try.

Shooting down the helicopters would be impossible with all the smoke and dust that filled the air, and with so many rockets still descending on the camp like guided thunderbolts. The best that he could hope for was to rescue someone, anyone, before the last of his *compadres* were wiped out.

How many had been killed already? Espinosa wondered. How could anyone survive such brutal fire? He told himself that it was only smoke that brought the hot tears to his eyes. He couldn't help thinking of the wives and children in the camp. Espinosa had no woman of his own, no children who would carry on his name, but he had come to love them all as fellow warriors in the struggle to redeem their homeland. Now, to simply stand and watch them die was more than he could bear.

Espinosa heard one of the helicopters swooping overhead and raised his carbine, firing through the smoke and dust. He had no target, other than a looming shadow and the whop-whop of the rotors, broken by the sudden rattle of machine-gun fire. The bullets weren't aimed at him. They were passing overhead to find some other target in the camp.

He kept on firing as the helicopter passed, then turned to face the next one, coming in behind it. *Damn!* If he could only see the pilot, get a clear shot through the gunship's windshield, he would give the bastards something to remember for their trouble. But there was no shot, and so the rebel emptied out the carbine's magazine in hopes the Virgin Mary might direct one of his bullets to the fuel tank or the engine, knowing even as the rockets thundered down behind him, that She hadn't heard his prayer.

Reloading on the run, Espinosa started for the trail bikes. He was no great motorcyclist, but he knew the basics. If he found one of the bikes still functional, perhaps he could escape, take someone with him. To fight again some other day. He saw the cycles, two sprawled on their sides, two others still erect and waiting on their kickstands. With a sudden rush of hope, he sprinted forward, breathing acrid smoke that burned his throat and lungs.

He never heard the rocket coming, with the clamor of explosions and erratic gunfire in the camp. One moment, he was lunging for the nearest motorcycle still intact, the next, it seemed as if a live volcano had erupted from the earth beneath his feet, hurling Enrique Espinosa skyward toward his adversaries.

He was dead before he hit the ground, riddled by shrapnel, seared by flame. And yet, from the expression on his face, a stranger might have thought Enrique Espinosa was relieved.

THE CAMP was burning. Bolan didn't need a local guide to tell him something had gone drastically, disastrously wrong. It had been thirty minutes since they left the jeep behind, concealed from all but the most tenacious searchers, and by Bolan's estimate, they still had a half mile left before they reached the rebel camp. They should be meeting sentries soon, assuming that the men in charge had any proper notion of security.

But then he sniffed the air and knew they were too late. No forest on the planet should smell naturally of gunsmoke, high explosives, burning oil and gasoline.

Too late, thought Bolan, as he paused and waited for a signal from his guides. Guillermo Cruz had smelled it, too, and Ariana Vasquez made a little gasping sound, as if she was about to cry.

Bolan set down the heavy duffel bag he carried, unzipped it and removed a CAR-15, the compact version of an M-16 assault rifle. He found a loaded magazine inside the bag and snapped it into place, chambered a round, then zipped the bag again and shouldered it, keeping the rifle in his hands.

He hadn't armed himself before because he knew Cruz would require some time to introduce him and to brief the soldiers in the camp about his mission. If he went in with a weapon showing, unannounced, it might have led to some unfortunate result. It made no difference now, however, since he guessed the soldiers they had come to meet were either dead or scattered through the forest, running for their lives.

There was no third alternative, he knew. Whether the raid had been conducted by the military or some "unofficial" death squad, the attackers would have come in force with ample guns and numbers to annihilate their enemies. It was the only way to play that kind of game, and the authorities in Panama—indeed, throughout Latin America—had been suppressing rebels for the past two centuries. Sometimes they failed, of course, in which case those who once were rebels suddenly became the new regime, and started to suppress their enemies.

Guillermo Cruz had drawn the Walther automatic from his belt and held it loosely in his hand, as if uncertain what to do with it. Beside him, Vasquez hadn't reached for the revolver that she carried underneath her denim shirt. Perhaps she reasoned that there would be no one left for them to fight. Bolan hoped she was right, but until he made sure, he was keeping the rifle in hand.

"How much farther did you say?" he asked.

Cruz answered him. "It may be half a mile," he said. "A little less, I think."

"I don't think there's a rush," said Bolan, "but we may as well go on as quickly as we can. With care, that is, in case they left someone behind."

Neither of his companions had to ask whom Bolan meant by *they*. Cruz and the woman had been living with the danger of arrest or worse for long enough to understand what must have happened to the camp, their friends. He was impressed particularly with the woman's fortitude. Dry-eyed, despite the moment of initial shock. She glanced at him and nodded, ready to proceed.

It took another forty minutes, hiking over rugged ground and pausing frequently to watch and listen, sniffing for potential traps. As they approached the former campsite, they were nearly overpowered by the stench of death and burning. Those were old, familiar smells to Bolan; they no longer sickened him, but neither did they make his day, as they did for some warriors he had known. The smell of napalm in the morning, to the Executioner, spoke less of victory than suffering and loss.

The camp had been wiped out. From what he saw, it was apparent that the strike had come by air, complete with plenty of rocket fire, tearing up the earth and dropping old-growth trees like they were pickup sticks. The tents and shanties had been blown away, their remnants charred and pocked with bullet holes—much like the bodies that were scattered everywhere. He turned his mind off when he saw the first child, disconnecting himself from his feelings, and he turned away as Vasquez lost it, kneeling in the dirt beside the twisted body of a girl no more than eight or nine years old. Guillermo Cruz moved like a zombie through the carnage, pausing now and then to stoop beside a body and confirm the loss of yet another friend.

The camp had once been fairly well concealed. Torn remnants of the camo netting still hung limply from a number of the trees that has been used as anchors. From the air, unless the rebels lit a smoky fire, Bolan surmised the camp would have been adequately screened from naked eyes. In which case, how had it been found?

There were at least three ways that he could think of without taking any special time to skull it out. An overflight with infrared could pick out campfires, generators, even body heat, providing a competent operator with a head count. He made a mental note to speak with Brognola to find out if the local military had such hardware in its arsenal, but even if the answer came back negative from Washington, it might be wrong. The Chinese People's Army could have slipped a little something to the Panamanians by now, besides their weekly bribes.

Then again, exposure could have come through plain bad luck. A rebel visiting the nearest town is recognized and trailed back to the camp, preoccupied with other things, oblivious to his shadow. Or a variation on the theme: a hunter, hiker or whatever stumbles on the camp, goes home and thinks about it for a while, then drops a dime to do his patriotic duty.

There was one more possibility, of course, and that

would be the presence of a traitor in the camp. Bolan suspected he was jumping to conclusions, since he didn't even know these people, and decided he would keep such speculation to himself. For now. Guillermo Cruz seemed wise enough to think of it himself, in any case, and Bolan guessed that he would think of little else for days to come, haunted by images of all his slaughtered friends.

The soldier gave them several moments more to grieve, then cleared his throat and said, "We shouldn't hang around. They may be coming back."

"To this?" When Vasquez spoke, she sounded breathless, weary, as if she had run for miles without a rest. "What for?"

"It's not uncommon," Bolan answered. "Blitz a target, fall back to an intermediate position, then rebound to look for any stragglers coming home. Besides," he said, voice softening a bit, "there's nothing we can do here anyway."

By that time, Cruz had found the final execution site where ten or fifteen rebels had been lined up in a row and shot with small arms at close range. Their wounds were different from the shrapnel scars and gaping holes that marked a .50-caliber machine gun's work. This last group had been executed in cold blood, without even the pretense of a "battle" underway.

"You're right," Cruz said. "We shouldn't stay."

"Guillermo…"

Cruz silenced Vasquez with a look, then turned to Bolan, hatred burning in his eyes. "We still have much to talk about," he said. "I have the names and other details that you need. Please help me kill the men responsible for this."

5

This time, the news that came to Colonel Bao Bai-fan by telephone was good. It didn't make him frown, didn't produce the burning in his stomach which he had begun to think might be an ulcer in the making. It was news, for once, that he was happy to pass on.

If there was any sour note at all, he found it in the fact that he must telephone ahead for an appointment with Lin Shao-pei. It was a mere formality. There was no question of Panama Harbor Authority's putative master refusing Colonel Bao an audience at any hour of day or night, and while Bao understood there were proprieties to be observed, it galled him all the same. It was as if he were required to ask permission for an order from some private in the ranks.

He could as easily have given Lin the news by telephone, but decades of clandestine service to the People's Revolution had ingrained a certain paranoia, which was, by now, an ineradicable part of Colonel Bao's personality. There were no scramblers on the telephones Lin used, and while there was no reason to suppose the Panamanians would eavesdrop on their conversation, Bao still feared other enemies might listen in. The CIA still had an active presence in the country, bland denials from the White House notwithstanding, and although America had formally renounced the days of gunboat diplomacy in Central America, Colonel Bao had no more faith in that declaration than he did in Beijing's latest promise to respect the human rights of Chinese dissidents.

By definition, what governments said and what they meant were two different things. It was understood, a simple fact of life. Some days, the colonel thought it was a miracle that the United States hadn't reacted to the presence of his countrymen in Panama with economic sanctions, even military force. It was ridiculous to think that no one in the CIA or at the Pentagon was conscious of the Chinese influence at work, or the strategic implications of a Chinese hand controlling the canal. Some nights, Bao lay awake in bed and asked himself, What are they waiting for?

But now, for all intents and purposes, it was too late. With absolute control of the canal reverting to the local government—a government malleable and corrupt the Americans would have a hard time selling the United Nations on a fairy tale that China had "invaded" Panama.

A Chinese secretary led him to the office occupied by Lin Shao-pei and then retreated, eyes downcast. For all his airs, at least Lin seemed to run his office with the proper discipline. His private egotism was another matter. It hadn't encroached on their relationship yet, and Colonel Bao knew how to deal with Lin, if such a thing should happen.

Lin Shao-pei was on his feet, circling around a massive teakwood desk as Bao entered the office. They didn't shake hands. Instead Lin nodded stiffly, not quite bowing, as he spoke in Cantonese. "Comrade, most welcome. Would you like something to drink?"

"No, thank you, Comrade."

It was understood that Lin wouldn't drink, once the colonel had declined, but still he kept his cautious smile. "What brings you to my humble office, Colonel?"

Not so humble, Bao thought to himself, examining the lavish furnishings, but kept the dour thought to himself. "I have good news," he said.

"Indeed! And what is that?"

"The office is secure?" Bao took another glance around as if expecting to find microphones taped to the walls.

"Of course," Lin said. "Your own men check it every second day."

Bao knew that of course, having ordered the sweeps himself. Still, he was never quite at ease in Lin's opulent office, never felt entirely safe. Lin was a businessman, despite lip service to the party and the People's Revolution. Bao couldn't help wondering how Lin Shao-pei would react if the CIA made him an offer.

Never mind. "The news is from Major Duende," Colonel Bao explained. "He has conducted yet another strike against the rebels. This time, he thinks they may be broken." Bao was careful to give Major Duende credit for the statement, nothing to suggest what he believed or disbelieved. If the major was wrong, as had happened before, no one could ever say that Colonel Bao Bai-fan had endorsed his mistake.

"That's wonderful!" said Lin, seeming truly pleased. But the smile slipped a notch as he added, "If it's true, of course. I mean it's wonderful if it's true."

"We'll have to wait and see," Bao answered noncommittally. "I hope he's correct, this time. If not, I may be forced to intervene myself."

That wiped all trace of the smile from Lin's face, but he didn't ask what Colonel Bao would do if he was forced to take a hand. Lin was too wise for that. He understood the value of ignorance in perilous situations, when nothing he said or did could affect the result. In such cases, it was best to be silent, leave the thinking to others.

After a moment, Lin said, "I hope it won't come to that, Comrade."

Bao nodded wisely and replied, "I hope so, too, Comrade. It would be most unpleasant otherwise."

ADOLFO QUINTANA was working on his fourth *cerveza* and watching a naked woman dance on the small stage before him, grinding her hips to a Spanish cover of some rock-and-roll production from *El Norte*. She was young and fit, light-skinned, with a seductive smile. Another time, Quintana would have been aroused, might have suggested to the owner of the tavern that he should arrange an introduction, but that night his thoughts were elsewhere.

It was never good when he was summoned by the major. Most of his instructions came from young lieutenants. Major Duende rarely soiled his hands, and when a meeting was required, it was the major's call, reserved for situations where he felt some extra pressure was required.

So be it. It was all Quintana could expect. He served a function in the scheme of things and was rewarded for his service, but the men who still wore uniforms were skittish when it came to being seen with him. Deniability was sacrosanct, even in Panama. Officials seen consorting with a leader of the death squads might expect that fact to surface in the media—if not the native press, perhaps some paper in *El Norte*.

Quintana hadn't always been a social leper. Once upon a time—and not so very long ago—he'd worn a uniform himself, with medals on his chest, and had been treated with respect. Indeed, as a captain of the state security police, he had wielded more raw power than some military officers who outranked him. It had been Quintana's call, within certain prescribed limits, to order arrests, detentions and interrogations of suspected subversives. He had decided who received the dreaded knock at midnight, who was caged and questioned without recourse to attorneys, who was brought into court and charged with real or imaginary crimes. On more than one occasion, he had been the final arbiter of who should disappear without a trace, as if the individual had never lived at all.

Times change, however, and that change was seldom for the good, in Adolfo Quintana's experience. Once Noriega was removed from power, his replacements at the helm had been obliged to dance when they heard someone from *El Norte* whistle "Yankee Doodle." Not that they were barred from hunting dissidents. Far from it. It was understood by all concerned that leftists must be hounded from the land at any cost. If they couldn't be handled quite so openly as under Noriega, there were still ways to achieve the same result.

It was the nuns who brought Captain Quintana down.

Their mission had been folly from the start, one of those fuzzy-headed projects generated by the church from time to time. It was foolish for three nuns from San Francisco to show up in Panama at all, much less align themselves with homeless street children and other wretched scum. Quintana hadn't ordered their arrest, and he most certainly wasn't a party to their rape by seventeen of his enlisted men, resulting in one woman's death and yet another's going mad. He gladly would have court-martialed the men responsible—did, in fact, shoot the sergeant who joined in the rape—but wasn't allowed a chance to make it right. The Yankee press was howling for justice and the buck stopped on Quintana's desk.

He had been spared a court-martial, at least, though it was understood he must resign at once, forego his pension and all benefits in order to avoid a prison term. Age thirty-six and he had been cast out, with no skills other than command and combat. He was living hand-to-mouth, his meager savings gone, when Major Duende sent a fresh-faced lieutenant to make him an offer Quintana couldn't refuse.

Even now, five years later, he still missed his uniform, the respect it had accorded him. But he had greater power now, with no laws to restrain him. He was free to strike at targets on his own initiative, as long as they weren't protected by a hands-off order, like the Triad *narcotrafficantes* and the penalty imposed was always death. There were no judges to obstruct him, no bleeding-heart lawyers to delay the inevitable. He was paid for his service to the state, his troops were armed with the latest available hardware, and all he had to do in return was perform certain favors for Major Duende upon demand.

Quintana nearly missed the major entering the tavern through the back door, coming around the bar as if he were just another patron returning from the men's room. Duende didn't wear his uniform, dressing down for the occasion in khaki trousers and a loose brown peasant shirt, tails worn outside his pants, no doubt to hide a pistol in his belt. The major saw Quintana, made a beeline for his table and sat beside him without invitation. The major smelled of Havana cigars and Chinese food, a combination whose irony wasn't lost on Quintana.

"So, Major," the one-time captain said, "what brings you to this part of town?"

Duende ignored him until the young waitress had taken their orders, then said, "You've heard about our raid, this afternoon." He didn't ask, assuming that Quintana kept up with the latest military news, and his assumption was correct.

"I did," Quintana said, because an answer was expected nonetheless. "How much of the report was true?"

Duende frowned, almost as if insulted, though both men were well aware of how some military "triumphs" were inflated by the press. Quintana couldn't recall a single press release in which the Panamanian defense forces ever admitted defeat. Even the American invasion and arrest of Noriega had been couched in terms of victory. They were thrilled to death that their former commander-in-chief had been dragged off to prison in *El Norte*.

"This time," Duende said, after a sip of beer, "the story is completely accurate. We took them by surprise, a major camp. There were no prisoners."

Quintana smiled at that. "These peasant bastards," he remarked, "always resist arrest. I've found that to be true, myself."

Duende let that pass and fixed Quintana with a steady glare, dark eyes like two gun barrels aimed across the table. "There is still a problem, though," he said.

"And, that would be…?"

"Guillermo Cruz, or course," the major said. "He wasn't in the camp. Which means, since your men missed him, he is still alive and still at large."

"What can he do?" Quintana asked. "One man—"

"We don't know that he is one man," Duende retorted, cutting Quintana off.

"But, you said—"

"That there were no prisoners," the major interrupted him again. "I never said all rebels in the goddamned country were inside the camp!"

Quintana felt the beer begin to bubble in his stomach, as if he had swallowed seltzer tablets. It was as he feared: the major had come out to deliver the bad news in person.

"I have people looking for him," said Quintana, breaking contact with the major's eyes. "But I can put more on it," he amended. "I can send them out tonight."

"Do that," Duende said. "We'll all feel better when this matter's settled. *Sí?*"

"*Sí, Jefé.*"

And Quintana wondered if he had time for another beer before he hit the streets.

DAVID LING didn't particularly miss Macau. What he did miss was the proximity to China, his ancestral homeland, laboring for half a century beneath the yoke of godless communism. David Ling was not a spiritual man, per se—in fact, most casual observers would have said he was a godless man—but he appreciated the traditions of his people, spanning the millennia, and hated the way in which a handful of political puppets had tried to reverse that great history. More to the point, they had tried to eradicate Ling and his friends in the process.

Before the advent of Mao Tse-tung in 1949, the several Triads had enjoyed a gentleman's agreement with the Chinese government. Premier Chiang Kai-shek himself had been a Triad member, though that fact was swept beneath the rug in most published histories of China. With Chiang in command it was always understood that free enterprise came first, before the huddled peasant masses whining for another bowl of rice. Those favored with the talent to survive and lead were given room to grow and prosper with the blessing of the state.

The Communists has changed all that. The peasants still got nothing for their trouble, naturally; in spite of all the sloganeering, they were worked like slaves under the new regime, burdened with new restrictions telling them what they must do, where they must live, how many children they could have. When all else failed, three million of them had been starved to death in a campaign to "modernize" the Chinese mode of agriculture.

None of that concerned a pragmatist like David Ling. He hated the pernicious Beijing government because its fifty-year campaign against the Triads had expelled his family from its home in Jinagxi province fifty years before, and much more recently had stripped him of his soft life in Macau. Ironically, now that he found himself in Panama, so far from home, the Reds found him a valuable ally and were pleased to take advantage of his business acumen.

Such rank hypocrisy was nothing new, of course. While executing Triad members by the hundreds in a string of gaudy show trials, Beijing's commissars had quickly come to terms with those they couldn't reach. China should profit from the opium that grew in Yunnan province, they decided, and who better to assist with turning poppies into gold than Chinese exiles driven from their homeland by the Reds? What better market for their poison than Americans in uniform who tried to stop the People's Revolution from expanding into Vietnam? And if the plague spread back to the United States, who in Beijing could help but recognize poetic justice?

"It's the Colombians," said Michael Chan, his second-in-command. "Guzman insists he needs more money, that his men are taking all the risks."

"That's rubbish," Ling replied. "We lost as many men as he did when the first three convoys were attacked. The last time, we had five men killed or wounded, while our friend in Medellin lost none at all."

"I have reminded him of that," Chan said.

"And his reply?"

Chan shrugged. "He's a Colombian. He'll believe what he believes, regardless of the facts. The bottom line is that he wants a larger cut."

"Of course he does." Ling understood such men, their boundless greed. Wasn't he one of them? The difference, as he explained it to himself, was all a matter of intelligence.

"I'm tired of Guzman," David Ling declared. "He has outlived his usefulness. Reach out to Rubio Madera in Cali. Be circumspect, but let him understand that we are interested in doing business if the price is right."

"First thing tomorrow," Chan agreed.

"Tonight," the triad chief corrected him. "It's early yet. Let's give Madera something he can celebrate while he's cavorting with his whores."

"And Guzman, David?"

"I'll speak with him tomorrow," Ling replied. "Perhaps he'll be reasonable." Ling saw Chan begin to smile at that. "If not," he continued, "then we must invite him to negotiate a new agreement. Draw him here, away from Medellin, where he maintains an army and controls the law."

"You'd kill him?" Michael Chan wasn't so much surprised as he appeared to be concerned.

"Why not? Who is Raoul Guzman that he believes he can disrupt a working partnership with new, extravagant demands? Perhaps he has been sampling his own product and cooked his brain."

"It'll mean war," Chan said.

Ling considered the possibility, then frowned and said, "I doubt that very much. Guzman is old and fat, a decadent embarrassment to younger men who serve him. There is one, at least, who wouldn't mourn his passing, I believe. Especially if he were helped to take the old man's place."

Chan smiled. "Shall I speak to Aguilar?"

"Not yet. Guzman will bring his aides along with him to the negotiations. When the time comes, Aguilar must not be harmed. Make sure our soldiers understand. Whoever injures Aguilar will die the old way, long and slow.

"I'll see to it," Chan said. "But if we're forging an alliance with Madera, why do we need Medellin at all?" he asked.

"There are two reasons," David Ling replied. "First, if we share the wealth between the two cartels, we thus contribute to a state of peace that benefits ourselves. And, more importantly, I've heard from Colonel Bao. The military say they've crushed the peasants who were preying on our shipments. Found them camping in the mountains somewhere, like a flock of children, and destroyed them all."

"You think it's true?" Chan asked.

"We'll know if they attack another convoy. In the meantime, we behave as if the way is clear from Panama to the

United States, with nothing to prevent us moving all the product we can get our hands on."

"We may drive the price down in the process, David."

Ling responded with a careless shrug. "I've learned two things from dealing with the round-eyes, Michael. First, they have a boundless appetite for personal corruption. There isn't one in a hundred thousand of them satisfied with what he has, be it his wife and family, employment, or his private stash of chemicals. Recall your history. When a reporter asked the labor organizer John L. Lewis what his union wanted, Lewis simply answered, 'More.'"

"What is the second thing?" Chan asked.

"That we control the flow of product, both cocaine and heroin. Once Aguilar in Cali joins our team, we shall control the pipeline that delivers eighty-five percent of all cocaine and forty-five percent of heroin to the United States. The shit they deal from Mexico can't compare with China white. As for the Turks and the Iranians, I am considering new ways to make their lives unpleasant in the months to come."

"I should know better than to doubt you," Chan said, smiling.

"Never be afraid to doubt," said David Ling. "It makes you cautious, helps you stay alive. Doubt everything, but never show your doubt to anyone outside this room."

Chan nodded understanding. "I must call Guzman," he said, and turned to leave.

"Yes, do that," Ling advised the empty room, when Chan was gone. "And let us hope he's as stupid as I think he is."

THEY HAD RETURNED to Vasquez's flat, circling the block three times before they satisfied themselves that there were no observers staked out on the quiet residential street. Of course, that only meant that there were none so clumsy that they lounged beneath the streetlamp on the corner or sat smoking cigarettes in dark sedans parked at the curb. It was impossible to say exactly where a watcher might be lurking—one of Vasquez's neighbors could be on the military payroll.

The rebels had taken a near-fatal hit in the mountains, though Guillermo Cruz assured him they still had enough troops in the field to mount at least a token retaliatory campaign. In such an atmosphere, he knew it was possible to let paranoia run rampant, imagining enemies in place where none existed, and he counseled prudence, extending the advice to himself as they approached Vasquez's apartment house.

No sirens wailed, no guns went off as they stepped from the jeep and made their way inside, Bolan lugging his hardware in the heavy duffel bag. That way if they were cornered he at least was guaranteed a fighting chance.

Inside, once they had double-locked the door behind them, Vasquez put a pot of coffee on and they returned to the small living room, settling into the same seats they had occupied that morning before their jaunt to the mountains. It had been a long, exhausting day but Bolan needed answers, information, if he was expected to proceed. Hal Brognola had been unusually vague on the players when they met in Arlington, and Bolan would require specific information to coordinate a battle plan.

"All right, let's have it," he instructed Cruz. "It's now or never. I need everything. You may as well begin with the Chinese."

Cruz took a scalding sip of coffee and began. "The leader of the Panama Harbor Authority, from all appearances, is Lin Shao-pei. He came to Panama about five years ago, presumably from China. I have no idea, you understand, if any of these names are true or false."

"Go on."

"From what we have been able to discover, Lin Shaopei's connection with the Chinese embassy is Bao Bai-fan, supposedly a cultural attaché from Beijing. I suspect he holds some military rank, perhaps with their intelligence service, but I have no means of learning more about him. In any case, he enjoys diplomatic immunity."

Not from me, Bolan thought, and made a mental note to run the names past Brognola and Stony Man Farm.

"Bao's immediate connection to our government is Ernesto Aguilar, the deputy minister of commerce and internal affairs." Cruz fairly spat the name out, as if it left a foul taste in his mouth. "He's a traitor who deserves to die."

"I'm guessing that he doesn't make the rules, though," Bolan said.

"The rules? Ah, no. You're correct. Our government is riddled with corruption, from top to bottom. The president isn't immune, nor any members of the legislature, judges, mayors, police. Sometimes I fear there may be no one we can trust to start afresh."

"There's always someone," Bolan told him, hoping it was true. In fact, he had seen systems so corrupt that nothing short of an all-consuming firestorm could blow the filth away. "Who manages the counterinsurgency units?" he asked.

"Major Miguel Duende." Once again, the name was spoken like a curse, with even greater bitterness this time. "He doesn't fight himself, of course. Rank has its privileges. Instead, he sends his soldiers out to massacre the people. Sometimes, if unusual discretion is required, he sends the death squads."

"Like this morning?" Bolan asked, referring to the abortive kidnapping. So much had happened in the past twelve hours, so many more people had died, that Bolan almost felt as if a new day should have dawned.

"The same," Cruz said. "They lack official status and are publicly condemned from time to time, but no one ever moves against the death squads. It's understood they draw their membership from ex-policemen and from soldiers who have been court-martialed, street thugs looking for a chance to rape and kill without reprisal."

"Are you sure it's ex-policemen?" Bolan asked. "None of them still on active duty?"

"None, as far as I can tell," Cruz said.

Bolan had made a private vow, at the beginning of his one-man war against the Mafia, that he would never kill a law enforcement officer, no matter how corrupt or brutal—even homicidal—he turned out to be in daily life. He had begun by viewing them as soldiers of the same side, albeit sometimes twisted in their hearts and minds from contact with the scum they had to handle every day, susceptible to various temptations of the flesh. And while a few had suffered injury at the Executioner's hands, some others were suckered into traps that led them to a prison cell, Bolan had kept his promise through the worst of it. He felt naive sometimes, the more he learned about corruption and depravity, coming to recognize that some lawmen were thugs before they took the job—that they became police specifically to loot and kill with virtual impunity—but he wasn't prepared to violate his own injunction, at this late date. If death squad membership was truly limited to *ex*-policemen, he was ready to regard the killers as fair game.

"And who heads up the death squad?" Bolan asked.

"If rumors are correct," said Vasquez, "it's a former captain of the state security police, Adolfo Quintana. He's certainly a member of the death squad, even if he doesn't truly lead. You may have heard the name. Some years ago, there was a scandal in the press. Three nuns from the United States were brutalized, one of them killed. Quintana's men were judged responsible. He was dismissed to pacify your state department.''

''No jail time?'' asked Bolan.

She shrugged. ''He didn't join in the atrocity himself—that time, at least. His court-martial was a publicity event. He may be out of uniform, but he enjoys the favor of our government, perhaps more than when he drew a monthly salary. He's their private executioner.''

Bolan was unaware he was smiling until Ariana asked, ''Have I said something humorous, Mike?''

He wiped it off his face and shook his head. ''I'm sorry, no,'' he said. ''Long day, is all. Now, if you've got locations for these people, we can get to work.''

And he was thinking to himself: One executioner deserves another, right.

Damn right.

6

Philip Hong had hoped he would be able to relax a bit after the army did its job and ran the peasant rebels down, but here he was again on guard duty. Of course, he understood the need for tight security around the drugs that were stacked and waiting in a warehouse.

The warehouse was in Balboa Heights, a southwestern suburb of Panama City, located within a half mile of the famous canal. The first week he arrived in Panama, Philip Hong had spent the best part of an afternoon watching ships pass through the locks of the canal, fascinated by the engineering of it all. Unfortunately, that had been the high point of his stay, before he understood that there was really nothing else to see or do in this backwater banana republic.

He had been in Panama for sixteen months that felt like years. The country had become his prison cell, the tedium provoking him to wish that something would go wrong, a small glitch on the radar screen to break up the monotony.

He hadn't counted on the raids that wiped three of their convoys off the map, of course. Nor, thankfully, had he been fool enough to give his daydreams voice, which definitely would have placed him on the suspect list and could have spelled his doom. It was a well-known fact that David Ling and those around him at the top had lost their sense of humor in the tropic heat, compelled to search for traitors once they started losing shipments in the mountains. There had been none to find, but two young brothers had been shot for skipping out on guard duty at the very warehouse where Hong now walked his beat, an Uzi submachine gun slung across one shoulder. No one would catch Philip Hong asleep when he had work to do.

Some work, he thought. Standing around watching crates of drugs inside an ancient warehouse, while mold sprouted from the walls. It might have been more interesting if he was assigned to guard the mold. At least the gray-green fungoid growth was doing something, methodically devouring the warehouse, inch by rotten inch. Hong had a fantasy that one day he would come to work, Uzi in hand, and find the place completely overgrown, like something in the horror movies where a creeping mass of sentient slime devours men, their homes and their machines. In this case, though, Hong knew the movie's ending: David Ling would send him in to get the precious drugs, and never mind if he was eaten alive.

Still, it might be worth it, just to see—

The first gunshots took Hong completely by surprise. It was a pistol, probably a 9 mm, but it sounded like a cannon in the morbid stillness of the night. Hong froze, swinging the Uzi up and clutching it against his chest, trying to get a fix on where the shots had come from. Damn it! Had they been inside the warehouse? No. The echo sounded wrong.

Outside. He glanced around and saw no one coming, even though there were three other men inside the warehouse. Three outside made seven to a shift, and half of them had walkie-talkie radios to summon reinforcements if necessary. Hong wasn't one of those equipped to call for help, and since none of his brothers came to join him, he set off to look for trouble by himself.

More shots showed him the way, two weapons this time, one of them full automatic, tearing up the night. The sounds were still outside, but growing closer by the moment as he neared the most convenient exit. It wasn't an accident, with two or more guards firing, and he wondered if the military raid that afternoon had really been successful, after all. The locals would never admit to failure; that much, Hong was certain of. He took for granted that certain rebels had survived and were retaliating for the raid against their mountain camp.

So be it. If they wanted action, Philip Hong would gladly show them—

The explosion plucked him off his feed and slammed him backward, hard against a row of man-high crates that held refrigerators from the States. Hong hit the floor, breathless, and brought his knees up to his chest, wheezing for air. Somehow, he had retained his death grip on the Uzi SMG. In front of him, a swirling cloud of smoke and dust obscured the doorway he had planned on using as an exit from the warehouse, slipping out to join the fight.

No hurry now, he thought. The fight had come to him.

Hong glimpsed a furtive movement in the smoke, a man's shape drawing closer, one arm batting at the acrid fumes, the other leveling some kind of weapon. He couldn't make out the face, but knew none of his Triad brothers carried high explosives or would use them on the warehouse if he did. Hong lurched into a seated posture, back and shoulders braced against the nearest crate, and framed the moving shadow in his sights.

A short burst from the Uzi sent his target reeling, pitching headlong through the smoke. The dying man collapsed within a dozen feet of Philip Hong, sprawled on his side, eyes blinking at the weapon that had brought him down. Despite the smoke and dust that swirled around him, Hong still recognized the oval face of Sammy Lee.

The second shape was there before he knew it. This one was a round-eyed stranger, all in black and hung with weapons, pointing one of them at Philip Hong. No matter. Hong was bound to try, redeem himself if possible or die in the attempt. It was a coin toss, nothing on the table but his life.

Hong swung the Uzi toward his second target, saw the muzzle flash already winking at him from his adversary's weapon, then he knew and saw no more.

PANAMA CITY wasn't large, as Latin American capitals went, but it still offered Bolan no shortage of targets. Between the Triads and Colombians, Chinese officials and the paramilitary death squads, Bolan could have used a squad like Able Team or Phoenix Force to back him up. He was alone, however, with the sole exception of Guillermo Cruz, and Bolan had insisted that Cruz limit his involvement to the role of wheelman, ferrying the Executioner from one mark to the next and otherwise remaining well clear of the line of fire.

Cruz didn't like it, but he did as he was told, reluctantly. When Bolan finished with the warehouse and came back to the car reeking of cordite, soot smeared on his face, the rebel had been waiting for him, looking dazed. He would have heard the shooting, but had been unsure how many Triad guns were stationed to protect the target.

"How many were...?" Cruz seemed to lose his voice and left the question hanging there, unfinished.

"Seven," Bolan said. "We need to go, now."

"Seven." Cruz repeated it as if the number was a concept new to him, somehow beyond his grasp. While they were sitting there, the warehouse blew from the plastique and incendiary charges Bolan had deployed to take out the narcotics stash. A fireball wobbled toward the heavens, trailing smoke.

"Madre de díos!" Cruz was shaken, even after all that he had seen and done.

"We need to leave right now," Bolan reminded him,

and in another moment they were rolling toward the second target on his list.

The Triads had infested Panama City like cockroaches, purchasing a score of local businesses as fronts, investing in hotels, apartment houses, sundry other real estate. Their main business was drugs, but Bolan knew from past experience that they would deal in any contraband available, from stolen art to weapons and illegal immigrants. Cruz had managed to provide him with a list of names and addresses—some of them commercial, others residential—and he meant to visit most of them before his work was done.

Next stop: a social club where Triad soldiers spent their evening hours off. It was his second choice because the drug stash he had incinerated at the warehouse had a multimillion-dollar price tag on it, and he knew that if he struck the soldiers first, the warehouse might be reinforced before he had a chance to get there. This way, if his secondary targets somehow got the word before he reached them, scattering to battle stations, he would still have hit his adversaries where it hurt them worst of all—in the wallet.

The club was called La Bamba, though the clientele of late was more Chinese than Panamanian. It featured dancing girls who doubled as hookers, with a small casino tucked in back. The Triad soldiers loved to drink and gamble, even when the liquor made them careless and they knew the odds were with the house.

This night he would introduce them to a whole new game.

"Drop me off in the alley," he told Cruz, "then pull around in front and wait across the street."

"You can't go in that place alone," Cruz cautioned him.

"It's safer that way than to leave an unattended car outside," Bolan replied. "You want some action, you'll see plenty if they spot you waiting for me."

If Cruz had an answer for that he kept it to himself. He drove the car down a dark, filthy alley, with battered trash cans spaced along the walls at irregular intervals. The headlights were off, but enough moonlight found its way between the buildings to let Bolan see rats scattering before the car, some of them as large as Chihuahuas.

Bolan stepped out into darkness, waiting for the car to disappear before he made his move. A quick check of his gear confirmed the Spectre submachine gun was fully loaded with a 50-round box magazine in place; ditto his sidearms, the Beretta 93-R in its Galco shoulder rig and the .44 Magnum Desert Eagle on his hip. He wore no overcoat to hide the weapons, the extra magazines that weighted down his belt or the frag grenades suspended from his combat harness. There were no stray witnesses out here, and once it hit the fan inside, there would be no way to conceal the fact that he was dressed to kill.

The Spectre was a relatively new addition to his arsenal, though it had been around for years. Italian made, the compact SMG was fourteen inches long with the metal stock folded, its unique four-column magazine nearly doubling the ammo capacity of standard submachine guns, and it fired from a closed bolt, double action on the first shot, thus allowing Bolan to carry the piece with a round in the chamber and the safety off. Its forward pistol grip improved control when firing full auto, at a cyclic rate of 850 rounds per minute.

La Bamba's back door was unlocked, and Bolan let himself in, passing the restrooms and the noisy kitchen unobserved, homing in on the main room of the tavern. Pausing in the shadows for a moment, checking out the place, he counted half a dozen Asian men lined along the bar with perhaps an equal number seated at small tables, the latter accompanied by young women in heavy makeup and skimpy costumes. Based on the racket he could hear, the gaming room was situated somewhere at the far end of the bar, just out of sight. He couldn't judge the unseen crowd with any accuracy by its noise but Bolan guessed there were at least another dozen soldiers tucked away in there.

Long odds, but they weren't the worst that he had played. The hardest part, he thought, would be avoiding damaging the hookers seated at the tables or the two nude women who were rubbing against each other on the tiny stage to Bolan's left. He hoped they would have sense enough to duck and cover. Bolan wouldn't fire on them unless one of them came up with a gun.

The party's over, Bolan thought, and stepped into the room, raising his SMG to sweep the soldiers along the bar. The Spectre sounded like a buzz saw ripping through sheet metal, but the range of sounds immediately blossomed to include exploding glass and shrill cries of pain and fear, the noise of bullets slapping into flesh.

His human targets went down in a row like tin ducks in a shooting gallery, and Bolan used one hand to brace himself, vaulting the bar and dropping out of sight before the Triads scattered at the tables could react effectively. A barrage of pistol shots flew overhead, some of the bullets smashing liquor bottles on the shelves behind the bar, while others pocked the stucco wall. The Executioner stayed low and powered toward the gaming room, some forty feet in front of him, a frag grenade already in his hand. He dropped the pin and held the safety spoon in place, prepared to make the pitch as soon as he was satisfied no innocent civilians were inside the room.

Some of the players were emerging as he reached the far end of the bar, and Bolan swept them with a short burst from his Spectre, firing one-handed, dropping two in their tracks and driving the rest out of sight. He scuttled forward, risked a glance around the corner before ducking back as semiauto pistol fire blazed from behind two gaming tables and a bank of slot machines.

The Executioner had seen enough. He made his pitch and counted down the seconds until detonation, bracing against the heavy impact of the blast. A cloud of smoke and dust erupted from the gaming room, and Bolan wore it like a cloak as he returned to face the Triad shooters he had left behind.

Don't start without me, boys, he thought. I came to play.

THE FIRST REPORT of violence in the city was relayed to Colonel Bao Bai-fan at 10:15 p.m., more than an hour after the attacks began. By that time, there had been three raids in different quarters, and the caller—Michael Chan, reporting on behalf of David Ling—informed the colonel that some thirty Triad soldiers had been killed or wounded in the flurry of attacks. There was no clue to the identity of those responsible, although one of the wounded in a cheap dive called La Bamba had described the man who shot him as a round-eye, possibly American.

Bao had expected some reaction from the States—had been surprised, in fact, that Washington was silent all this time—and still the sudden violence took him by surprise. He had anticipated protests filed through diplomatic channels, possibly some saber rattling from the Pentagon, which might proceed to summit talks about the Chinese role in liberated Panama. If Washington pursued the challenge, they could argue points of law and etiquette for months on end at the United Nations while the Panamanian president and members of his cabinet weighed in on China's side, expressing gratitude for so much new investment capital. It would be foolish and embarrassing, at that point, for Washington to try gunboat diplomacy; worse than embarrassing, in fact, since the rest of the UN Security Council was sure to line up on China's side of the debate, defending Panama's autonomy.

But this! the colonel thought. What could it mean? Would the United States risk so much bad publicity by staging raids within Panama City this way, attacking civilians and gunning them down in the streets? It was a reckless move, even by old-style CIA standards from the adventuristic 1960s.

Unless...

Bao wondered if he might be mistaken in assigning blame for the attacks. He had only the secondhand testimony of one wounded gangster to confirm the race of one assailant, glimpsed in one of three attacks.

But why would an American attack Triads in Panama, if he weren't employed by the United States as a provocateur? Two other possibilities came instantly to mind, and neither of them put the colonel at ease. He knew that the narcotics traffic funneled into the United States through Panama was having an effect on prices and available supplies. The once-proud Mafia would feel that pinch the worst, and while La Cosa Nostra had been whittled down of late by federal prosecutions in the States, Bao had no doubt the capos still had men and guns enough to field a strike force, if their blood was up.

A second possibility, though more remote, concerned the possible employment of mercenary fighters by the decimated peasant rebels. Colonel Bao considered it unlikely, but he couldn't rule it out. There were unquestionably men of arms, including former British and American commandos, who regretted the passing of the Cold War, longing for another chance to try their luck against the Reds. With Russian communism gone, that left China as a focal point of rage.

Colonel Bao knew he was spinning his wheels, tormenting himself with notions that ranged from barely plausible to patently bizarre. The best thing he could do was go home and rest, enjoy a drink and wait for news of any more attacks. It wasn't his job to help the Triads fight for turf in Panama. If David Ling couldn't defend himself, he had connections in the local army and the death squads to assist him. Bao Bai-fan was an observer, nothing more.

Bao buzzed his driver on the intercom and ordered his car to be made ready. He spent five minutes tidying his desk, more for the driver's benefit than from any need to clean up, and then locked his office door behind him, moving toward the stairs. There was no elevator in the Chinese embassy, since the building was only four stories, including the basement bomb shelter. Most days, Colonel Bao enjoyed the exercise of walking up and down the stairs to his second-floor office, but this evening he was too distracted to think of such things.

The embassy stood on four acres of land, surrounded by an eight-foot wall with tangled razor wire on top. The limousine, an armor-plated black Mercedes-Benz, was waiting for him when the colonel stepped outside, humidity hitting him like a slap in the face after the air-conditioned atmosphere within. Suppressing an urge to curse the climate and the country as a whole, he nodded to the soldier on the door and moved toward the limo, where his driver and bodyguard stood flanking the open rear door.

Bao didn't hear the first shot coming, but he witnessed its effect, up close and personal. One moment his personal bodyguard was nodding to him, not quite smiling, and the next his head exploded like a grapefruit with a firecracker inside. Bao flinched away and had his eyes closed when the blood splashed his face, small chunks of scrambled gray matter adhering to his cheeks and jacket, clinging to his hair.

The echo of the shot came through a heartbeat later, when the colonel was already diving for the safety of the armored limousine. Bao glimpsed his driver turning foolishly in the direction of the noise, awestruck, before a second bullet drilled him through the forehead and his cranium was airborne, pouring its crimson on the pavement as he fell.

Bao landed facedown on the floorboard of the Benz, hands trembling as he swiped away the blood that stung his eyes and blurred his vision. He tried to keep from retching at the salty taste of the blood that had found its way inside his mouth.

Two bullets struck the limousine in swift succession, but the armor held. From their apparent placement, judging by the sound, Bao guessed the sniper hadn't meant to strike him, even if the shots had penetrated glass and steel. What then? Was this a message? Were they playing mind games? Would it be a war of nerves?

The colonel clenched his fists to stop his hands from trembling. There were no more shots and he heard embassy soldiers rushing toward his car, glanced back to see them crouching as they moved around the bodies on the pavement, brandishing their automatic rifles in the air. Damned fools! Who would they fire on, when the enemy was perfectly invisible.

Bao made no move to leave the car, though he thought better of returning to his house in the suburbs. This night, it would be wiser if he slept inside the embassy. Besides, he still had work to do.

The colonel had to plan his own moves in what promised to become a dirty, costly war.

LEAVING THE EMBASSY behind him, Bolan reckoned it was time to let the Chinese have a breather while he checked in with the local death squad. If his plan for general disruption of the drug-and-politics cartel had any chance of working, he would have to rattle all the players, keep them guessing the identity of their assailants and—ideally—provoke violent dissension in the ranks. That wouldn't be achieved if he neglected any of the players, and he didn't want the local goons to feel left out.

He had considered starting at the top, targeting Adolfo Quintana, leader of the death squads, but Bolan had reconsidered the plan, deciding he'd rather face Quintana, the known quantity, than some anonymous replacement whose background and temperament were a total blank. Accordingly, he now directed Cruz to drop him at another address, this one on the south side of the city, where an empty building waited for him in the dark.

Like most other terrorist movements, the Panamanian death squad operated in the shadow of a noble-sounding front group, the Crusade for Public Decency. A squat two-story building in an old commercial district served as headquarters and an effective clearinghouse for information filtered off the streets. Ostensibly, the CPD was apolitical, supporting any candidate who vowed to rid society of crime. In practice, it endorsed the current president despite his obvious corruption and the fact that widespread criminal activity had flourished under his administration. Pamphlets and inflammatory speeches were the movement's public stock-in-trade, but its clandestine operations were of more concern to Bolan at the moment.

In the past ten years, the death squads had kidnapped, tortured, and murdered Panamanian civilians at an average of one per day. Some of the victims had been petty criminals, a few of them drug dealers who had offered competition to the smugglers favored by the government in power. Others were beggars and homeless, their sole offense embarrassing a regime that prided itself in a facade of affluence. The majority, meanwhile, had been political dissenters, those courageous or foolish enough to attempt reform of the system by constitutional means, through debate, petition and civil disobedience. When all else failed, a few—like those who joined Guillermo Cruz—had turned to force of arms.

The CPD headquarters was unoccupied at night, except on Tuesdays, when weekly meetings were held in the assembly hall. This was Thursday night, and while Bolan expected no opposition, he still went in ready to fight, armed with the Spectre and both handguns just in case. Approaching from the rear, he found the back door locked and spent a moment with a pry bar to defeat the simple dead bolt. There was no alarm, the death squad's arrogance assuming no one in his right mind would attempt to vandalize CPD property. Bolan moved through the darkened rooms at will, depositing his parcels here and there, the timers synchronized. He had ten minutes, start to finish, and was out in half that time, jogging back to the car where Cruz had parked it, well down the block.

"That wasn't so bad," Cruz remarked, as Bolan slid into the passenger's seat.

"Not so bad," Bolan agreed, before the night turned into noonday, half a dozen thermite bombs erupting simultaneously in the building up the street. He watched the white-hot flames consume it from within, smoke pouring through the melted windows, blanketing the neighborhood.

He checked his watch and found it was 11:25 p.m., still early when it came to stalking predators who prowled by night. "You tired?" he asked his driver.

"Tired? No, no," he said. "Not tired."

"Good deal," the Executioner replied. "Let's roll."

7

Ariana Vasquez understood why Cruz and the gringo, Mike Belasko, wanted to keep her out of the action. It was all part of the whole machismo mind-set, two men telling one another that they were protecting her while neither of them thought her capable of doing anything to help. She had grown up with men who held such attitudes, beginning with her father and her uncles, then her brothers, finally the husband who had shared her life too briefly prior to disappearing inside one of Noriega's prisons where he lost his life.

So she knew all about machismo, and she held it in contempt. If anyone had asked for her opinion, Vasquez would have told them that women were the backbone of the resistance movement, standing by and offering support to those who fought, no matter what went wrong, in spite of all the burdens they were forced to carry, simply by virtue of their birth. And women did fight in the movement, though perhaps not in the same way men were called upon to fight. Instead of creeping through the jungle dressed in camouflage and carrying machine guns, they were called upon to wheedle information out of drunken men, sometimes to lead their "dates" a certain way, along a certain street. She knew a woman—well, had known her; she was gone now, executed by the death squads—who had worn a razor strapped against her thigh, beneath her peasant skirt, and who had slit the throats of half a dozen soldiers while they literally had their pants down.

Vasquez had no wish to play that part, but after what the three of them had seen that afternoon, the slaughter in the mountains, she couldn't be satisfied standing on the sidelines, mouthing slogans while the marching army passed her by and disappeared from view. She must do something for the cause. But what?

The radio reported bombing incidents and shootings, scattered throughout several quarters of the city. Vasquez reckoned that must be Cruz and Belasko working through their list of targets from the death squads and the Chinese gangsters who infested Panama. She wished them well, but simply knowing they were out there fighting made her need for action that much greater.

Finally, in something close to desperation, she got dressed again, went out and locked the door behind her as she left. She didn't take her car. She preferred to walk. If she accomplished nothing else this night, at least she could burn off some nervous energy. The .38 revolver tucked inside the waistband of her new designer jeans was something of a comfort as she walked along the sidewalk with its long dark stretches between the streetlights, moving restlessly, without a clear destination.

When she had walked for some three-quarters of a mile, she realized where she was going. It didn't surprise her and she smiled, pleased to discover that her female intuition was alive and functioning.

The club was called El Matador. The Killer. There was irony in that, she thought, since it attracted many officers from the security police, and some reputed members of the death squads, too. "Reputed members" simply meant that no one kidnapped by the death squads ever lived to point a finger at the men responsible, and since no member of the execution teams had ever been arrested, much less prosecuted, no one who participated in the daily crimes was truly "known." Even the man in charge, Adolfo Quintana, wore a mask in public, posing as a spokesman for the proud Crusade for Public Decency.

She almost had to laugh at the notion that a decent world could be constructed on the bones of countless murdered victims. It was sick, a travesty.

Why was she going to El Matador? That part of it was still a little hazy in her mind, but Vasquez reckoned she could drink a beer and have a look around, perhaps strike up a conversation with a soldier, glean some information from him that was useful to the cause. Or she might sit quietly and eavesdrop on the young men as they boasted of their raid this afternoon, pick out some targets for reprisal in the days ahead. Whatever. Even if she only had the beer and learned nothing at all, at least it was a deviation from routine, a chance to get away from her apartment on this night when there was murder in the air.

She was still four blocks from the club when a dark sedan passed her, heading in the opposite direction. She heard the car make a U-turn in the middle of the block, its headlights washing over her. It pulled up close behind her, slowed to walking pace. Though Vasquez longed to bolt for cover, she wouldn't allow herself to run. She didn't want to jump to conclusions. It could be rape or just a stranger asking for directions. Then again it might turn out to be the death squad.

"Ay, chica!"

Someone was calling to her from the car. She kept on walking, playing deaf and dumb, until she heard the brakes squeak and a door popped open. When she stopped and turned to face the man now standing on the sidewalk, counting three more in the car, she honestly expected nothing, but feared everything.

"I know you, don't I?" asked the young man on the

sidewalk. He had military bearing, but was decked out in civilian clothes.

"No," she replied. "I don't think so."

"You look familiar," said the stranger. "Come and take a ride with us."

She shook her head, placing one hand on her hip, a little closer to the two-inch .38.

The stranger dropped his smile. "You hurt my feelings, *chica*. And I really must insist."

Inside the car, someone shifted, then she saw the muzzle of a weapon poking up behind the driver's seat. Without another moment's hesitation, Vasquez drew her pistol, thumbed the hammer back and fired.

She didn't shoot the stranger standing on the sidewalk, had no real desire to kill or injure anyone. She fired into the windshield of the dark sedan, between the driver and the empty shotgun seat. She was rewarded with a crash of glass and angry curses from the other passengers. When Vasquez swung her weapon toward the lone pedestrian, he raised his hands and flinched away from her, a furious expression masked by sudden fear. He had to hurt her now, if he survived. He had to repay her for the damage to his pride.

She turned and bolted, racing down an alley, hearing shouts and footsteps behind her. They would have to send the car around to head her off; the alley was too narrow and too cluttered for a vehicle to pass. Escape depended on her speed and courage. If she was only swift and brave enough....

She spun and fired again, aiming for the human silhouette that followed her, this time knowing a hit would be unlikely. The pistol shot was loud inside the alley, its muzzle-flash dazzling. Vasquez turned again and plunged ahead.

An instant later, she was facedown in the dirt, gasping

PLAY
RUN
FOR THE
ROSES

and get
THREE FREE GIFTS!

HOW TO PLAY:

1. With a coin, carefully scratch off the silver box at the right. Then check the claim chart see what we have for you — **2 FREE BOOKS** and a **FREE GIFT**—**ALL YOURS FRE**

2. Send back the card and you'll receive two hot-off-the-press Gold Eagle® novels. These books have a cover price of $4.50 or more each in the U.S. and $5.25 or more each in Canada, but they are yours to keep absolutely free.

3. There's no catch. You're under no obligation to buy anything. We charge nothing — ZERO — for your first shipment. And you don't have to make any minimum number of purchases — not even one!

4. The fact is, thousands of readers enjoy receiving books by mail from the Gold Eagle Reader Service™. They like the convenience of home delivery...they like getting the best new novels months before they're available in stores... and they love our discount prices!

5. We hope that after receiving your free books you'll want to remain a subscriber. But th choice is yours — to continue or cancel, any time at all! So why not take us up on o invitation, with no risk of any kind. You'll be glad you did!

This surprise mystery gift
Could be yours **FREE** –
When you play
RUN for the ROSES

PLAY
RUN FOR THE ROSES

Scratch
Here
See Claim Chart

YES! I have scratched off the silver box. Please send me the 2 FREE books and gift for which I qualify! I understand that I am under no obligation to purchase any books, as explained on the back and opposite page.

RUN for the ROSES	Claim Chart
♛ ♛ ♛	**2 FREE BOOKS AND A MYSTERY GIFT!**
♛ ♛	**1 FREE BOOK!**
♛	**TRY AGAIN!**

NAME (PLEASE PRINT CLEARLY)

ADDRESS

APT.#   CITY

STATE/PROV.   ZIP/POSTAL CODE

366 ADL C25V

166 ADL C25U
(MB-OS-05/00)

The Gold Eagle Reader Service™ — Here's how it works:

Accepting your 2 free books and gift places you under no obligation to buy anything. You may keep the books and gift and return the shipping statement marked "cancel." If you do not cancel, about a month later we'll send you 6 additional novels and bill you just $26.70* — that's a saving of 15% off the cover price of all 6 books! And there's no extra charge for shipping! You may cancel at any time, but if you choose to continue, every other month we'll send you 6 more books, which you may either purchase at the discount price or return to us and cancel your subscription.

*Terms and prices subject to change without notice. Sales tax applicable in N.Y. Canadian residents will be charged applicable provincial taxes and GST.

If offer card is missing write to: Gold Eagle Reader Service, 3010 Walden Ave., P.O. Box 1867, Buffalo NY 14240-1867

BUSINESS REPLY MAIL
FIRST-CLASS MAIL   PERMIT NO. 717   BUFFALO, NY

POSTAGE WILL BE PAID BY ADDRESSEE

GOLD EAGLE READER SERVICE
3010 WALDEN AVE
PO BOX 1867
BUFFALO NY 14240-9952

NO POSTAGE
NECESSARY
IF MAILED
IN THE
UNITED STATES

for breath, her weapon gone, lost when she fell. She couldn't believe it. She had tripped on a beer bottle. She tried to rise and run but she seemed to have no strength. Her arms and legs had turned to rubber; they wouldn't support her weight.

The stranger stood above her, breathing heavily. He called her filthy names, but she was still surprised when he drew back and kicked her in the ribs. The second time she saw it coming but couldn't protect herself. After the fourth or fifth kick, thankfully, the pain became too great to bear, and she lost consciousness.

"I'M STILL NOT certain why you let the Chinese colonel live," Guillermo Cruz remarked, as they approached another target on the hit list. "You're clearly not afraid to kill. He wields great power in this city, in the nation."

"There's your answer," Bolan told him. "I'm going for a divide-and-conquer strategy. For that to work, there has to be someone in charge of the contending sides. Right now, the colonel's wondering who wants him dead and why. With any luck the next few moves will have him looking at his partners in a whole new way."

Cruz smiled. "You worked this out very quickly."

"Things come to me," the Executioner replied. "Is this our address, on the right?"

The target was another gambling club, but this one was different. Club Rio was a Triad operation run for profit, as opposed to La Bamba, where the soldiers went to play. No member of the Triad was allowed to drink or gamble on the premises. Their presence on the scene as management and muscle was, in fact, thinly disguised by hiring locals to front the operation, offering a Latin flair to Panamanian players and tourists alike. The club was high-toned in comparison to the dive Bolan had raided earlier, with some serious money on the tables. That, in turn, created both an opportunity and a problem for the Executioner.

This was Bolan's chance to hit the Triads where they lived, albeit not as badly as he had by torching their narcotics stash in Balboa. The problem was Club Rio's clientele, made up of innocent—if gullible—civilians who were simply out for a good time. He couldn't turn the club into a free-fire zone, as might have been possible if it was frequented primarily by thugs.

Therefore, a compromise.

Bolan had dressed for the occasion, stopping off along the way to slip on a suit and dress shirt, the jacket cut to hide the 93-R in its armpit rig. He also wore a lightweight overcoat this time, in stark defiance of the muggy temperature, to hide the Spectre submachine gun that he carried in a simple shoulder sling. The pockets of the overcoat were weighted down with military smoke grenades, making it look as if the Executioner had put on twenty-five or thirty pounds around his hips. If his attire raised any eyebrows on the street or in the club, he was confident that he could manage to distract the gawkers with a fireworks show.

"Wait here, unless the cops show up," he said to Cruz, and left the car a half block from Club Rio, moving confidently toward the doorway framed by garish neon. Just inside the door a bouncer and a pretty hostess greeted him together.

"Good evening, sir," the hostess said in perfect English with just the barest trace of accent. "May I take your coat?"

"No, you may not," Bolan replied, and let her see the Spectre, rising in a swift arc from its hiding place, the muzzle sweeping up and over toward a hard collision with the bouncer's face. The guy was staggered but he tried to shake it off. It took a swift kick in the groin to put him down, but Bolan figured it was better than a Parabellum round between the eyes.

The hostess was about to scream when Bolan turned and brought the muzzle of his SMG to rest beneath her dimpled chin. Slight pressure, and her white teeth clicked together, biting off the sound of panic that was building in her throat.

"You're closing for repairs," he told her, smiling. "I'd prefer that nobody gets hurt. You want to help with that, stand by and do your job. Or you can hit the street right now. There's no third option you'll enjoy."

The lady blinked at him and answered through clenched teeth. "I'll help," she said, the accent more pronounced as fear made her forget some of her elocution training.

"Fine. You'll have a rush here, pretty quick. Just help them get outside as rapidly as possible."

"All right."

He thought of frisking her for weapons, but the sequined dress she wore was tight enough to rule out underwear, much less a hidden gun. He turned away from her, stepped past the bouncer curled up on the floor and made his way inside the club, a smoke grenade already primed and ready in his left hand, Spectre in the right.

He lobbed the OD canister in the direction of the stage where a quartet was slaughtering some tune by Lennon and McCartney. After about six seconds, a crimson cloud of smoke erupted from beneath a roulette table, where the fat grenade had come to rest. Immediately, screams and curses filled the air, almost eclipsing Bolan's shouts of "Fire!"

There was a risk that someone would be injured in the rush, he knew, but they were safer on the run than remaining in the midst of what might soon become a battlefield. So far, he had seen no Triads and that was fine. If they were all off somewhere else, engaged in other business, he would be content to trash the club and leave. But if the club had gunners hiding somewhere in the woodwork, he would have to deal with them as they appeared.

A second smoke grenade was spewing yellow clouds behind the bar and a third was airborne toward the middle of the dance floor, when the first triad defender showed himself. Bolan wasn't sure where he came from, probably a lounge or office in the back, but with the stampede under way and colored smoke filling the air, he hadn't marked the soldier's first appearance on the scene.

No matter. Bolan had him now. The shooter tried to nail him with a shiny semiauto pistol from the far side of the room. His first two shots were high and wide, drilling the ritzy wallpaper, and Bolan didn't let him have the opportunity to try again. A short burst from the Spectre stitched a line of tidy holes across the gunman's chest and slammed him back against the bar, legs buckling as he slipped into his final pose.

One down, and the reports of gunfire sped the frightened gamblers on their way. One guy in a tuxedo had been scrambling for chips around the roulette wheel, but he forgot them now and sprinted for the nearest exit, elbowing the players who had gotten there ahead of him. Bolan was tempted to unleash another short burst toward the ceiling, but he held his fire, conserving ammunition, just in case he needed it for living targets.

Two of those showed up a moment later, bulling through the smoke from what appeared to be a hallway leading toward the restrooms, storage space, whatever, at the far end of the bar. One of the new arrivals was Chinese and had a sawed-off 12-gauge pump; the other was Hispanic, almost certainly a local, and he had a long-slide automatic pistol in each hand.

There was no reason to announce himself or give his adversaries the first shot. This wasn't Hollywood, and he wasn't obliged to play by any rules that jeopardized his chances of survival. Bolan strafed them with a burst of Parabellum manglers from a range of twenty feet and dropped them in their tracks before they saw it coming. Quick and clean, the way he liked it…if he had a choice.

Bolan moved through the smoke, checking behind the bar, then moving on to scan the back rooms for stragglers. A rear door stood open, spilling light and smoke into an alleyway, marking the exit route of someone who had opted for discretion over valor. There was no one in the office, no one in the toilets, no one in the storeroom where the booze was stacked in cardboard boxes.

Perfect.

Bolan left his first incendiary with the liquor stores, where it would find no end of ready fuel. He dropped another in the small, untidy office, knowing it was overkill, but wanting to make sure he got the business records, plus whatever cash might be concealed there. By the time he got back to the club's main room, the whole place was deserted, no one but the three dead men to see him drop a final thermite canister behind the bar.

All done.

Cruz had the motor running when he got back to the car, and didn't wait around this time to watch Club Rio burn. "Do you enjoy this?" he asked Bolan, after they had driven for another mile or so in silence.

Enjoy it? How should he begin to answer that one, short of pouring out his whole life history? "Just drive," he said and concentrated on the mental hit list, working out his next stop of the night.

"WE HAVE TO do something!" So angry was he when he shouted out the last two words, that a thick, wormlike vein pulsed visibly on the left side of Adolfo Quintana's forehead.

Ricky Muñoz tried to pacify his master, knowing it

would be a critical mistake for him to smile at the moment. "We are doing something, Adolfo," he said, in his best calming tone. "We have teams out patrolling the streets, a hundred men or more. Major Duende can't suggest that we are sitting on our hands."

"Major Duende can 'suggest' whatever the hell he wants to," Quintana retorted. "And it doesn't matter if we have a thousand men out on the streets. So far, they haven't seen or done a thing to help resolve this situation. Am I right, Ricky?"

"Well..."

"It's bad enough we have to help these Chinese at all. Now, when they need us, if we can't even do that, what good are we to anyone?"

"Adolfo, we weren't—"

"And our own headquarters, dammit! By the Blessed Virgin, how are we supposed to hold our heads up in this city, if we can't protect our own damned headquarters?"

"There was no reason to expect—"

"'No reason to expect?' Is that your answer, then?" Quintana's tone was scornful. "We wage endless war against the scum of Panamanian society, and there's no reason to expect they might retaliate? Of course not! Who in his right mind would ever think of such a thing?"

A flush of angry color tinged Muñoz's cheeks. "You may recall, Adolfo, that we spoke of posting guards around the building. A year ago," he said. "You found the notion pointless. I believe you said it was 'a silly waste of time and manpower.'"

"I see. It's my fault, now." Quintana seemed to have regained control. Ironically the change from shouting to a low-pitched snarl made him sound even more dangerous than before.

"Of course not," Muñoz backpedaled. "I only meant to say—"

"Enough!" Another shout. "I want no more excuses, explanations or Hail Marys. Understand? I want results! Someone is making war against the Chinese, and they've included us. I don't know what that means, yet, but I will know, and when I find out, the bastards will regret the day that they were born."

"I wonder," said Muñoz, cautiously, "if there might not be more than one person responsible."

Quintana hesitated, blinking at his second-in-command. "Explain yourself," he ordered.

"Well…" Muñoz was hesitant, seeming to know that if he said the wrong thing now, he might be leaving through the back door in a body bag. "The Chinese were attacked first, as I understand it," he went on.

"So?"

"What if those who struck at them aren't the same *pendejos* who attacked our headquarters?" Muñoz said.

"Speak plainly. This is no damned time for riddles."

"I just wonder if, perhaps, the raid against us may have been retaliation for the strikes against the Chinese," Muñoz suggested.

"What? We have done nothing to the Chinese," Quintana said. "Why would they turn on us, unless…you mean…?"

"Two possibilities," Muñoz said, with somewhat greater confidence. "The first is that someone in the Triad leadership believed we were responsible for the attacks on them."

"Ridiculous!" Quintana scoffed. "We have protected them since they concluded their agreement with *El Presidenté*."

"It's unlikely, I agree. Although who can fully understand the workings of the Oriental mind? Another possibility, however, is that someone in the Triad saw an opportunity and took advantage of it. Striking while the iron is hot, as gringos like to say."

"What opportunity?" Quintana asked. "You make no sense."

"The Chinese think of nothing but themselves, their profits," Muñoz said. "They care no more for Panama than for the other nations they infest." He saw Quintana nodding, agreeing with him in their common prejudice and forged ahead. "Suppose they saw an opportunity to cut us out and keep the money they would otherwise have spent on our protective services? If they pretended we had some part in the raids against their property, their actions would be justified, and they could logically refuse protection in the future, using their own men exclusively."

"Suppose you're right," Quintana answered, sounding skeptical. "That still doesn't explain who is attacking the Chinese."

Muñoz shrugged. "It could be anyone. Colombians, perhaps."

Quintana shook his head. "They are in bed with the Colombians."

"Maybe no one has attacked them, after all."

"I know you're crazy, now," Quintana said. "Major Duende has been touring the scenes, himself. The warehouse in Balboa, all their drugs, that club—what was it called?"

"La Bamba," Muñoz said. "I'm not suggesting there has been no violence, Adolfo. Maybe—just maybe—the Chinese had to clean house, some private matter in the ranks, and those who have been killed were sacrificed. As for the drugs in the Balboa warehouse...well, who saw them, after all?"

"You mean...?"

"I mean that little can be told from ashes, and Duende won't be running any tests to prove that there were drugs inside the warehouse when it burned. That would embarrass his *compadres,* if the news got out. He acts on what the Chinese are telling him, Adolfo."

"Wait," Quintana said. "Somebody tried to kill their big man from the embassy, the colonel."

"Someone shot his driver and his bodyguard," Muñoz replied. "From what I understand, the sniper was extremely skilled and had a clear shot at the colonel, but he chose a couple of subordinates instead, and let the big fish get away. That doesn't sound like any serious attempt to me."

Quintana's frown was carving furrows in his face, like dueling scars. "And who is it you think did this?" he asked. "The goddamned Triads take their orders from the Chinese embassy."

"In theory, yes," Muñoz said. "Again, there are two possibilities. It's well known that mainland China has suppressed the Triads, even if it still makes use of them abroad, from time to time. Large numbers of them have been shot or thrown in prison. There is no love lost between the Triads and the Chinese government."

"So they attempt to kill the colonel who employs them and protects their drug trade here and then decide to miss on purpose? I believe you've lost your mind, Ricky."

"As I said—" Muñoz remained unshaken by the criticism "—there are two potential explanations. First, Triads may have staged the incident in hopes that Colonel Bao Bai-fan will question our ability, the state's ability to guarantee security within the capital or in the countryside at large. A second possibility, the Triads and the colonel may have worked it out together, as a scheme to make us look inept and justify whatever moves they make against us, claiming self-defense."

Quintana brooded over that for several moments, silently, and when he spoke again, his voice was somber, with a certain chill. "You've given me a lot to think about," he told Muñoz. "I'm not convinced that your suspicions are correct, but I'll take what you have said into account.

Meanwhile, I say again, we must do something in the face of these attacks or we become a public laughingstock.''

"I humbly await your orders, *Jefé*," Muñoz said, without a hint of mockery.

"Pick up one of the Chinese," Quintana said. "No one important, necessarily, but someone who might know if there were any schemes afoot involving us. I also want our men to pick up any stragglers from the rebel forces they can find and question them in depth. As for the rest...I'll have to think about it."

"*Sí*, Adolfo. As you say, it will be done."

I hope so, thought Quintana, when he was alone once more.

He hoped that something would begin to go his way, and soon, before it was too late.

THE HOME OF Lin Shao-pei wasn't initially designed with personal security in mind. Of course, it was constructed for a wealthy man, which meant that it was located in one of Panama City's best neighborhoods. That in itself insured a measure of police protection which the populace at large would never see. Aside from the police, some residents of the exclusive neighborhood had pooled their resources to hire a private security firm, armed men in off-the-rack uniforms who drove around in year-old cars with stylish badges stenciled on the doors. Essentially, they watched for vagrants, beggars and the like, checked vacant houses while the owners were away on holiday and sped to the scene with lights flashing in the rare event that an alarm went off.

As luck would have it, Lin Shao-pei didn't subscribe to the private security service. He preferred to trust the mighty combination of his government—that is, the People's Republic of China, as personified by Colonel Bao Bai-fan—and in the colonel's various connections with the Triads, the security police, and any extralegal forces otherwise included in the mix. Lin was a cautious man, however, and because he had sufficient wealth, he had taken some precautions of his own. An eight-foot wall of stone surrounded his home and two acres of land. The wall had shiny nails and broken glass on top, set in cement. Closed-circuit television cameras, mounted at each corner of the property surveyed the house and grounds from four directions.

The wall prevented any passersby from staring into windows on the ground floor of Lin's house. That hardly mattered on this night since his private study occupied a southwest corner of the second story, facing toward the street. Lin hadn't thought to purchase special glass to ward off sniper fire. What was the point?

Across the street and one house down, there was a vacant home. It had been offered up for sale a few weeks earlier, the owners transferred off to Venezuela in a corporate shift of personnel. The local rent-a-cops drove past it once or twice a night, checking for lights inside that would suggest a thief at work or squatters on the premises, but it wasn't priority.

Bolan approached his setup from the rear, across a spacious yard that could have passed for Hollywood, if there had been a swimming pool. He picked the backdoor lock instead of smashing it, in case the rent-a-cops decided it was time to stop and walk around the homestead, rattling doorknobs. Once inside, he used a penlight briefly to locate the stairs and find the second-story roost that he was looking for.

His weapon for this mission was a Walther WA-2000 sniper rifle. Futuristic in design, with a gas-operated bullpup assembly, the Walther fed six rounds of .300 Magnum ammunition from a detachable box magazine seated behind the pistol grip. The rifle measured only three feet, end to end, and twenty-six inches of that was barrel set in a straight line from the sniper's shoulder, externally fluted to minimize vibration, rigidly clamped to the frame at front and rear to prevent the torque of bullets passing through it from lifting the muzzle in combat. The weapon's Schmidt & Bender telescopic sight made Bolan feel as if he were inside the room with Lin Shao-pei, instead of watching him from sixty yards away.

The Walther wasn't fitted with a sound suppressor, although he had one in the duffel bag beside him, on the floor. It was a judgment call, and Bolan had decided he would take his chances with the neighbors, in lieu of tampering with the Walther's proven accuracy. In any case, since he was using supersonic ammunition, with a muzzle velocity exceeding 2,900 feet per second, any effort to muffle the gunshots would bear mixed results, at best.

He found his spot, opened the window, sitting well back in the room so that a passerby couldn't glance up and see a rifle barrel braced across the sill. He used a straight-backed chair that had been left behind, along with sundry other furnishings, to brace the Walther's bipod while he marked his target, peering through the telescopic sight into the world of Lin Shao-pei.

The man was seated at his desk, smoking a cigarette and fussing over paperwork. He seemed distracted, which was only natural. By now, the Executioner surmised, Lin had to have heard about the local raids—some of them, anyway. He was a close associate of Colonel Bao Bai-fan and shared important business interests with the Triads, and both had taken hits within the past few hours. Bolan couldn't read the stranger well enough to know if he was worried or frightened, but he watched Lin shuffling through his papers, setting them aside, then reaching out for them again, as if he sought some pressing answer hidden in between the lines.

Lin jumped, and Bolan wondered what had startled him until his target reached out for the telephone that occupied one corner of his desk. Lin spoke into the mouthpiece, listened, spoke again, eyes narrowing to slits, his mouth set in a line that may have telegraphed distaste or simple anger.

More bad news?

You ain't seen nothing, yet.

Bolan shifted his aim, allowing for deflection by the window glass on impact, found his mark and stroked the Walther's hair trigger. The rifle bucked against his shoulder but he rode it out, watching glass shatter across the street, seeing the telephone jump off Lin's desk yanking the handset from his grasp as it exploded in midair.

Round two was sighted on a framed photograph, arranged to face Lin from the left side of his desk. Bolan couldn't see the photo, and he didn't need to. He was counting on the fact that anyone whose likeness occupied Lin's desk was near and dear to him, a face whose mutilation by a Magnum round—even on paper—would give the Chinese wheeler-dealer cause for second thoughts.

Round three burned through the headrest of Lin's high-backed chair, the man himself already slumping toward the carpet, whether in a swoon or conscious effort to protect himself, the Executioner could not have said. It hardly mattered, either way, since Bolan did not plan on killing Lin Shao-pei that night. This visit was a wake-up call, nothing more.

He pumped the last three rounds into the massive wooden desk in rapid fire, careful to aim high, since he couldn't tell where Lin was hiding underneath. Two seconds more, and he had stashed the Walther in its duffel bag, backtracking through the house and out into the yard.

The neighborhood was waking up around him, lights winking on here and there in formerly darkened windows. Bolan hit the back fence running and was over in a flash, gliding along beside another house with an attached garage, no sounds of agitation from inside. Another fifteen seconds, and Guillermo Cruz pulled to the curve, waiting for Bolan as he stowed the bag and slid into the shotgun seat.

"Did it go well?" Cruz asked, when they were rolling.

"Well enough for me," Bolan replied. "I think our buddy Lin may have a different point of view."

"What's next?"

"I want to let things simmer for a little while and see what happens. Is it safe for us to stop at Ariana's place again?"

The smile on Cruz's face bespoke relief, and something more.

"It should be safe enough," he said, and urged a bit more speed out of the sedan, retreating toward the barrio.

8

The pain was everything. At first it had been fierce enough to steal her consciousness, and now it showed persistence, nagging at her until Ariana Vasquez twitched and sobbed her way back to the waking world.

Her ribs hurt the worst, the left side of her torso where her kidnapper had slammed his heavy boots so zealously. Slumped over in the chair she occupied, she had unconsciously put extra pressure on her injured side, the sharp pain jolting her awake. She wondered if her ribs were broken, noting that although it hurt to breathe, there was apparently no damage to her lungs from jagged bones.

Her next impression was a combination of the chill and the smooth, hard contact of a wooden chair against her back, buttocks and thighs. Before she even glanced down at her body, Vasquez knew she was naked. In another moment she confirmed that she was tightly bound to the chair, secured with heavy duct tape at her elbows, wrists and ankles, while a narrow chain was looped around her waist and clamped or locked somehow behind her back. In terms of movement, she could shift uncomfortably in her seat—a painful effort in itself—but that was all.

Someone had beaten her unconscious, brought her here and had taken off her clothes, then taped and chained her in the chair. What else had happened, while she was unconscious? Vasquez didn't feel as if she had been sexually violated, but her thoughts were still disjointed, a ferocious headache merging with the pain of battered ribs, the lesser aches and scrapes of falling in the alley, being dragged and tossed around like so much baggage, so she couldn't rule out anything with certainty.

Where was she? Biting off a whimper at the pain the movement caused her, she craned her neck from left to right, surveying roughly half the room in which she was confined. It was a fair-sized chamber, twenty feet across the end that she could see, although she couldn't calculate how deep it was behind her. When she cleared her throat the echo made her guess the room was sparsely furnished, possibly with nothing but the chair in which she sat. There was no carpet on the concrete floor, no doors or windows in the walls of concrete blocks that she could see. The door must be behind her, and she imagined it was shut, since she could hear no sounds from anywhere outside.

A soundproof room? There was no insulation on the walls, but Vasquez didn't know how such things were constructed. She had no idea if she was underground or in some chamber of a labyrinthine prison, though the chill suggested distance from the muggy night outside. There was no air-conditioning, however, and the room was stuffy, even though its temperature raised goose bumps on her naked flesh.

She was afraid. Of that there could be no doubt whatsoever. Vasquez had grown up with stories of the state security police and what they did to prisoners, particularly dissidents. A thief might simply go to jail and serve his time, but those who questioned the almighty workings of the state were likewise questioned in their turn, required to give up names, addresses, bits of information that incriminated friends and kin. Some of those detained for questioning would simply disappear without a trace. The ones who made it home again were never quite the same, jumping at shadows, always frightened, cringing from the slightest human contact. Vasquez had known some of them, since she enlisted in the movement, and she sometimes thought the dead were luckier than those who managed to survive.

It struck her, then, that she might be unduly optimistic, guessing that her captors represented the police or military. There was yet another possibility that offered no hope whatsoever of survival. If she had been taken captive by the death squad, there could only be a screaming hell of suffering that ended with her mutilated body dumped along some roadside, maybe planted in a shallow forest grave.

Too late for worrying, she told herself, and wondered from the harsh pain in her throat if she had said the words aloud, unconsciously. She thought the beating might have shaken something loose inside her head, and knew that she would have to keep her mouth shut once they started on her, do her best to keep whatever secrets she possessed locked inside.

There wasn't much, of course. She knew about the campsite in the mountains, but it had already been destroyed. Likewise, she knew Guillermo Cruz's name and address, but she couldn't tell her captors where he was this night. No matter what they did to her, no matter how she suffered, Vasquez couldn't give up secrets she did not possess.

What else?

It hit her, then: the gringo, Mike Belasko. If her enemies weren't aware of him, his presence in the city, what he planned to do, that information could be critical. It might just be enough to save her life, in fact, but Vasquez caught herself before she could pursue that train of thought. Better to die than sell her soul, and there was no good reason to suppose her captors would keep any promise made to her, in any case.

How best to keep her secret, then? If no one asked about Belasko or a gringo stranger working with the rebels, it should be a relatively easy task. The great temptation, once they started hurting her again, would be to volunteer the information, offer it in trade to stop the pain. They might be grateful for the gift, appreciate her generous cooperation and release her.

Or they might just blow her brains out where she sat.

Best not to tell, if she could possibly resist. Belasko meant to help them, she was sure of that, and if she gave him up, what would the cost be to her own immortal soul? Her personal attachment to the church had waned of late, but not her faith in God. How would she face His judgment as a traitor to the cause of human rights and freedom?

Vasquez was still pondering that question when she heard a door scrape open several yards behind her. A cool draft raised new goose bumps on her skin, and she could feel the short hairs bristling on her nape as heavy footsteps made their way across the concrete floor.

MAJOR DUENTE hated being rousted out of bed at midnight to resolve some problem of his subordinates. It rarely happened these days since rank had its privileges, unless guerrilla forces were rampaging through the capital itself. The situation this time was less critical, but Duende, after studying the naked woman for a moment reckoned that his underlings were wise to call him after all.

She was a looker, this one, even battered as she was, and while she stirred him, Duende was—for once—more interested in her mind than in her luscious body. Ariana Vasquez was a known friend, and lover, of Guillermo Cruz, the rebel who had managed to elude his own men and Quintana's with such seeming ease. With some persistence and a little luck, Duende just might learn where Cruz was hiding. All he had to do was ask the woman, in a manner she couldn't ignore.

He stood in front of her, at ease, his hands clasped behind

his back, and made no secret of studying her body. When he met her eyes at last, Duende saw the spark of fear that he was hoping for, although she did her best to hide it from him, putting on a bold mask of defiance.

"Señorita Vasquez, I believe," Duende addressed her in a quiet, conversational tone. The screaming would come later, from the woman in the chair.

"Why have you brought me here?" she asked.

"I think you know the answer to that question," he replied. "You're involved in various subversive acts against the state that jeopardize our national security. Your friends—the ones who still survive, that is—are hunted men. Eventually, I'll have them all, as I have you tonight. How long that takes and how much they are damaged in the process may be something you can help me with."

She arched her back a little, proud breasts rising in defiance. "You believe that I would help you kill my comrades? You must be a fool," she said.

"And yet," Duende answered, smiling his refusal to be baited, "I'm not the one bound to a chair without my clothes. I'm not the one who looks as if he had been mistaken for a soccer ball." He paused, then added, thoughtfully, "I'm not the one who must consider whether I'll live to see another day."

"Better to die with honor than to live in shame," the woman said.

"Of course. It says that in the storybooks." Duende paused again and studied her. "Where is the glory in a filthy, screaming death, when all the time you know your comrades will be mine in time, despite your sacrifice? Why die in agony? Indeed, why die at all when there is nothing you can do to save them?"

"There is always self-respect," she said, her voice a bit subdued this time.

"Ah, self-respect. The dictates your decision, then? I

wonder what your self-respect will feel like when you vomit from the pain and can't hold the contents of your bowels? Won't that be glorious? A moment you can cherish, on your way to hell.''

"We make our own hell," Ariana Vasquez said. "A traitor spends his whole life there.''

"A problem you may not be called upon to face," Duende told her, with a mocking smile. "Still, I'll do my best to make your final hours—or days—as hellish as I can. We're quite adept at this, you know. Just when you're certain that it can't get any worse…it does.''

"I have nothing to tell you," she replied.

"How curious. We've never spoken, you and I, and yet you take for granted that there's nothing in your life that I don't know about? You flatter me, Ariana." Another pause, before Duende said, "Perhaps we should begin with your good friend, Guillermo Cruz.''

"I never heard of him.''

Major Duende's laugh was genuine, spontaneous. This would be pleasant, after all, a labor well worth losing sleep. "Of course you don't," he said. "How silly of me. Still, we must be certain.''

When he snapped his fingers, two young soldiers came into the room, one pushing a stainless-steel cart in front of him, the kind often seen in hospitals and dentists' offices. The second soldier pushed a mover's dolly with a large truck battery attached, thick insulated cables slung across one shoulder, each end capped with shiny alligator clips. They wheeled the cart and dolly to a point in front of Vasquez's chair, a few feet to the major's left, and waited for his nod before they left the room. One of them closed the door behind him as they exited.

"Most often, I would leave these chores to a subordinate," Duende said, "but I believe in setting an example for my men from time to time. It helps morale. I'm sure you understand such things."

As Duende spoke, he lifted a white towel that covered an array of tools and implements neatly arranged on the wheeled cart's top shelf. She saw a corkscrew, scalpel, pliers, ice pick, scissors, tweezers, metal skewers, sewing needles and a compact butane torch.

"Not very subtle, I'm afraid." The woman tried to cringe away from him as he stepped closer but she had nowhere to go. "Another time," he said, "we might have used drugs, perhaps hypnosis, but such things take time which I can't afford to waste just now. You will forgive my sad reversion to more primitive techniques, I trust. They're quite effective, after all."

"Can they extract knowledge that I don't possess?" she asked him, fighting to control the tremor in her voice.

"A question worth considering," Major Duende said. "Of course, there's only one way to find out. Shall we begin?"

"Go to hell!"

"Another time, perhaps." Duende smiled, his fingers moving restlessly along the shiny row of instruments. "For now it's your turn. I'll be your tour guide."

THE PLACE WAS DARK when Cruz drove past the first time, checking on the left side of the street for lookouts, while Bolan scanned the right. Two circuits of the block and they were satisfied that no one lay in wait for them, no soldiers crouched in alleyways or huddled in cars along the curb. Cruz parked the car a block away, though there were places nearer the apartment house. Bolan took his bag of weapons with him as he left the car, and they walked back together through the dark.

Upstairs, Cruz used the knock they had agreed on: two taps, then one, immediately followed by two more. It was a simple code, but nothing their enemies were likely to divine by chance. They waited on the landing, heard no sound within, and when a second knock brought no response, Cruz felt a cold dread in his stomach.

"She could be sleeping," Bolan said, but something in his voice told Cruz that he didn't believe it. If she had dozed off, Cruz thought, it would be in the living room. More likely, she would be awake and waiting for them, pacing like a tigress in a cage.

"I have a key," he said at last, and fumbled in his pocket for it. He had never used the key before, but there was no good reason why the American should know that. Let him assume that Cruz and Vasquez were romantically involved. Why not?

His hand was trembling as he turned the key, then edged the door ajar and stuck his head inside. Calling her name, he stepped across the threshold, with the gringo warrior close behind him. Cruz didn't require a tour of the flat to know they were alone, but they went through the motions anyway, and came back to the tiny parlor empty-handed.

"Anyplace she might have gone?" Bolan asked. He was concerned, although he did his best to hide the fact.

Cruz shook his head, drawing a mental blank. "The stores are closed," he said. "She's not a drinker. I suppose she may have gone out for a walk, but..."

"Well," Bolan said, "there's nothing to suggest that she was taken out of here by force."

Cruz recognized the truth of what he said. The door revealed no signs of damage, and it seemed unlikely that kidnappers would have locked it when they left. If there had been a struggle in the flat, neither the furniture or decorations had suffered damage. Vasquez's bed was neatly made, her kitchen counter clear and spotless, dated magazines stacked neatly on her coffee table, corners perfectly aligned.

Cruz willed himself to breathe, relax and concentrate. If she had gone out voluntarily, despite the hour, she might still return unharmed. It troubled him that she had left no note behind, despite the fact that she had been expecting their return. Was it a simple oversight or something far more sinister?

Cruz looked around the room again, feeling stupid simply standing there. He should be doing something, going somewhere, seeking help. The sudden sense of loss was overpowering, as if a frigid hand had thrust itself between his ribs and torn his heart out.

Where would Ariana go?

There was no answer to the question, since he couldn't read her mind. Perhaps, if they *were* lovers, Cruz would stand a better chance of trying to predict her movements. As it was, though…

Suddenly, he realized that he was asking the wrong question. Since he couldn't think for Vasquez, couldn't crawl inside her mind, he must attempt to think like someone from the other side. If she was taken by their enemies, where might she be?

There were two possibilities, of course. If she had been taken by the death squad, then she was beyond all hope. It was too late to help her, even now. Her body would be found, or not, depending on the whim of her assassins. There was nothing he or anybody else could do, except try to avenge her once her fate had been confirmed.

There might still be a chance, however, if she had been taken by the state security police. Cruz tried to picture how it could have happened, Vasquez stepping out for some reason, an agent or informant spotting her, making the grab or trailing her and calling reinforcements. If she had been taken from the flat, the place would be a shambles, more than likely under guard. That left the streets, and since her car was still downstairs, that meant she had been walking somewhere when they took her by surprise.

Still speculation but it was all Cruz had to work with. It remained his only reasonable hope that she was still alive. "I need to use the telephone," he said, Bolan watching him but keeping quiet as he made his way back to the bedroom, reaching for the phone on the nightstand, close beside the bed that they had never shared.

His contact with the state security police was named Ramon Cervantes. He was twenty-six years old, employed as a dispatcher and occasional file clerk at headquarters. He had enlisted with the rebels fourteen months before, after his younger brother was arrested by mistake and beaten so severely that he wound up crippled, feeble-minded and babbling nonsense like an infant all day long. Cervantes did the best he could at grievous peril to himself, supplying information from the files, occasionally tipping off the rebels to a scheduled raid, twice managing to name informers in the ranks who later disappeared without a trace.

Cervantes worked the night shift. He was at his desk when Cruz got through to him and used the code name they had prearranged. "It's Bolivar," he said. "I need your help."

There was risk involved, of course. According to some rumors, the security police eavesdropped on phone calls even in their own headquarters, but he trusted that Cervantes would be conscious of such things and would protect them both.

"I'm glad you called," Cervantes said, Cruz wincing as his stomach tightened in a knot.

"It's Eva," he continued, using Vasquez's code name.

"*Sí,* I know." There was a moment's hesitation. In his mind's eye, Cruz could see Ramon Cervantes checking out the squad room, making sure that it was safe to speak.

When he resumed, his voice had lowered almost to a whisper. "She was taken off the street tonight."

"Taken by whom?" Cruz asked, his eyes clenched tightly shut against the sudden burning there.

"Major Duende's men," Cervantes said. "They plan to question her. I think they've probably begun by now."

"Where can I find her?"

"I don't know," Cervantes answered, sorrowfully. "I'm not told such things, you understand?"

"All right," Cruz said. "If you hear anything at all—"

"I'll call at once, of course."

Cruz hung up cradled the receiver, walked back to the living room on legs that felt like lead, and found Bolan watching him.

"They've got her."

BOLAN HAD BEEN there before. Not in this place, but in that frame of mind evoked by peril to a comrade, be it a long or short acquaintance, who is placed in danger by association with his personal crusade. This time there was a difference, of course: the war had been in progress when he got there. There was no reason for him to feel responsible for anything that happened to the players as a proximate result of their dissent.

And yet...

He blocked that train of thought before the blame game could distract him any further, concentrating on the odds that Ariana Vasquez was alive. Cruz's source had verified her pickup by the state security police. With the death squad, it would simply be a body search, no hope at all of finding her alive. This way, at least, there seemed to be a fighting chance.

And Bolan guessed that he would have to put the emphasis on fighting.

It was one game he knew how to play. The enemy had

something, someone that you wanted, and no amount of slick diplomacy would do the trick. Possession was nine-tenths of the law, and he who held the cards controlled the game...unless the opposition grabbed him by the throat and rattled him so viciously the cards slipped from his trembling hands.

Bolan knew better than to lead with threats. So far, the opposition didn't know he was in town, had nothing more than vague descriptions of a gringo striking at them without warning, then fading back into the night. He could be anyone, a soldier representing any faction from the Mafia or CIA to the proverbial "persons unknown." Uncertainty was one of Bolan's weapons, and he meant to use it well. His strikes around the capital had been designed to dazzle and confuse the enemy, set one paranoid faction against another. Next time he would need to leave a message, loud and clear. He would repeat the message time and time again until it reached someone with the authority to give him what he wanted.

After that the end result would be in someone else's hands. Major Duende's? Someone higher up the food chain? Bolan didn't know, and he didn't particularly care. He meant to turn up the heat, bring the cauldron to a boil and force his adversaries to release the woman. They had to come to understand that only by conceding this specific point, could they achieve some measure of security. While Vasquez was detained in hostile hands, the city would remain a free-fire zone. No one would be safe.

The game plan was a risk, of course, for all concerned. On Bolan's end, it meant maximum exposure in pursuit of a distinctly limited objective. He had known Vasquez for less than twenty-four hours and had no reason to believe that her survival was critical to the resistance movement in Panama. Some would have asked him why he bothered, when he had so many other targets on his list...but those who asked the question would be strangers to the Executioner.

More critical than any danger to himself, he had to think about the risk his actions posed to Vasquez. He was squaring off against a group of men—or several groups—for whom brute force and violence were the first resort, a recognized solution for all kinds of problems, ranging from the trivial to the extreme. That very afternoon, Major Duende of the state security police had ordered the annihilation of a village, including its women and children, with no more hesitation than he might have showed while stepping on an anthill. What did one more woman matter in the scheme of things?

There was a chance, Bolan admitted to himself, that his attempt to rescue Ariana Vasquez might precipitate her death. Of course, she could be dead already, in which case the whole campaign would be a waste of time, but Bolan had to find out for himself. And he could still seek vengeance. Or if the bastards panicked, maybe opted to retaliate for Bolan's strikes by killing her—there would be hell to pay in Panama.

"I'll need your help on this," he told Guillermo Cruz.

"Of course."

"I don't mean driving," Bolan said. "I need to leave a message when we hit-and-run. That means you'll have to come along and fight."

"I've fought before."

"You stand at least a fifty-fifty chance of being killed," the Executioner informed him, driving home the point.

"They've taken Ariana," Cruz replied. "What shall we do?"

"We finish off our list of targets," Bolan said, "but concentrate for now on those related to Duende and the state security police. Each stop, we let them know the heat stays on full blast until they give us what we want."

"Will they kill her?"

"It's a possibility," Bolan admitted. "I won't lie to you. There is a chance they'll do exactly that."

"And if we don't try…" Cruz let the sentence trail away, his eyes downcast.

"If we do nothing, then they win," said Bolan. "You'd know more than I about the number of detainees who survive abduction and interrogation by Duende's people."

"Ariana won't survive," Cruz said. "She will defy them to the last. They'll have to kill her."

"There's your answer, then."

"But if we fail…what then?"

"We live with it," the Executioner replied, "and pay them back in kind. We kick ass either way, as long as we're alive."

"I need to make a stop and pick up some equipment," Cruz remarked.

"Sounds reasonable," Bolan said. "Let's go."

9

Guillermo Cruz had retrieved his M-1A1 Thompson sub-machine gun from its hiding place in a commercial storage facility, along with spare magazines and a quantity of .45 ACP ammunition. The weapon had survived his leap into the river six weeks earlier, a testimony to the rugged manufacture that had seen it used successfully in combat from World War II through the recent wave of ethnic cleansing in the former Yugoslavia. His stash of clips included four 30-round magazines, two shorter 20-round mags and one of the rare 50-round drums made famous—or infamous—in American gangster films. Together with the Walther semiauto pistol in his belt, Cruz now felt adequately armed to face his enemies and try to rescue Vasquez from their clutches.

Bolan had surprised Cruz by declaring that he wouldn't kill a member of the state security police. Cruz saw no logic in it, but he acquiesced to the suggestion that they strike at targets linked to Major Duende, one way or another, while leaving pointed messages behind at every stop. If Duende didn't release Vasquez, alive, the raids would continue indefinitely, heaping financial loss upon the major's allies—and embarrassment upon Duende—until he gave in.

Or until he killed Cruz and Bolan.

That possibility hadn't escaped Cruz, but he refused to dwell on it, preferring to contemplate victory. How sweet it would be to see Vasquez again, to know that he had rubbed Major Duende's nose in the foul stench of failure. And if he got the chance to target Duende himself...well, Cruz shared none of the American's scruples when it came to killing enemies in uniform.

Their first target in the new wave of attacks was a penthouse apartment downtown where a Colombian dealer named Jorge Rochon had his headquarters. Cruz parked behind of the hotel beside an overflowing garbage Dumpster where he estimated that the car wouldn't be stripped or otherwise disturbed within the time allotted for their raid. He had removed the Thompson's wooden stock, and it fit easily beneath the raincoat he wore, the pockets heavy with spare magazines. He led the way inside, Bolan on his heels, and they stood waiting for the service elevator.

It was after midnight, still not late by Hispanic standards. Restaurants around the city would be crowded, nightclubs waiting for the dinner crowd to finish eating and begin their rounds in search of liquor, sex and other diversions. The hotel, meanwhile, was winding down, most of its daytime cleaning staff already gone home, a skeleton crew on hand to deal with room service or any minor emergencies. Cruz and Bolan had the service elevator to themselves as they rode all the way to the top.

"Remember," said Bolan, when they still had two floors left to go. "We need someone to carry the word, preferably someone with clout."

"I promise not to kill Rochon unless he makes me angry," Cruz replied.

"It works for me," Bolan said, and smiled.

The elevator stopped, its door hissed open and they stepped into the corridor, guns sliding out from underneath their coats. Bolan's weapon was a smaller, lighter submachine gun, but Cruz liked the Thompson's solid weight and its proved stopping power. He had killed with it before and would again before the night was out.

As if in answer to his silent thought, two long-haired men in dark suits appeared before them, blinking at the SMGs as they reached for weapons underneath their tailored jackets. Bolan took the shooter on their right, a short burst ripping through his chest, while Cruz chopped down the second man, his heavy .45 slugs spattering the wall with gore.

They rushed the penthouse door, Bolan squeezing off a burst that blew the knob and dead bolt clean away, nothing to stop him when he hit the shattered wooden panel with a flying kick and bulled his way inside. Two more Colombians were standing in the middle of the spacious living room, each with a pistol in hand, and in the split second before all hell broke loose, Guillermo Cruz had time to wonder why these drug traffickers always seemed to wear their hair like women.

The long-hairs were raising their pistols when Cruz and Bolan opened fire, the Thompson's chatter almost drowning out the lighter sound of 9 mm Parabellum fire. The bodyguards each got off two or three rounds as they fell, rounds wasted on the furniture, at least one bullet drilling through the ceiling. Cruz was glad that they were in the penthouse, no neighbors upstairs to be killed in their sleep or while watching TV.

Two bedrooms opened off the main room of the penthouse, one on either side. They split up, with Bolan breaking to the left, Cruz to the right. There was no sound in either of the rooms at first, but then a woman screamed from Cruz's room, the rising shriek cut off abruptly with a sound of knuckles meeting flesh.

Behind him, Bolan checked the other bedroom, found it empty and immediately doubled back. They flanked the doorway of the darkened room, both crouching, in case Rochon was armed and started shooting through the walls.

Bolan reached inside his coat and palmed a fat grenade

resembling a beer can painted olive drab. He pulled the pir and warned the Panamanian, "Eyes and ears."

Cruz shut his eyes and cupped his palms over his ears as his companion tossed the stun grenade into the bedroom Seconds later when it blew, he felt as if a giant hand had slapped him on the back with more than friendly force.

They rushed into the smoky bedroom, found Jorge Rochon sprawled on the floor beside his king-sized bed. A naked woman huddled on the mattress, breathing fitfully, a livid mark beneath one eye revealing where Rochon had punched her moments earlier.

They dragged the dealer into his living room, Cruz slapping him until it seemed that he could focus with his bleary eyes, responding to simple questions when Cruz shouted loudly enough. They showed him his dead soldiers and prodded him with the still-warm muzzles of their guns. Rochon decided that he would, indeed, prefer to live.

"You know Miguel Duende, from the state police?" Cruz asked.

"Miguel?"

"Major Duende, idiot!"

"Oh, yes. I know him."

"We have a message for him. You're the messenger."

"A message?" Hope flared in the dealer's eyes. "I'll tel him anything you want," Rochon said, eagerly.

"The woman, Vasquez," Cruz continued. "Say her name."

"The woman, Vasquez."

"She must be released, alive and well. And soon!"

"Alive and well. I'll call the *maricon* right now!"

"Do that," Cruz said. "And then get out of Panama You're no longer welcome here."

THE SECOND TARGET called for somewhat more finesse, bu it was worth the effort. Reaching out to touch a member of the presidential cabinet who had connections both to the security police and to the Triads would provide a graphic demonstration that no one in the city—no one in the country—was immune to punishment if their demands remained unmet.

Selection of their second target had been relatively simple, ironing out the basic details no great challenge, but the Executioner was still concerned. He recognized that he was walking on a razor's edge, demanding critical concessions from a man whose uniform—and Bolan's private vow—made him immune to any lethal action on the soldier's part. Of course, Major Duende didn't know that, although Bolan had felt honor-bound to brief Guillermo Cruz on his personal pledge to refrain from killing policemen. Cruz accepted it with equanimity, though it was clear he wouldn't mind eliminating Duende and the rest of the security police himself, if given half a chance. And if it came to that, would Bolan try to stop him?

No.

The choice to kill or not to kill in any given situation was a matter of conscience. Bolan wouldn't knowingly fire on police, corrupt or otherwise, but he wasn't duty-bound to protect them either, if they strayed beyond the limits of their lawful authority to maim and terrorize.

They were in position, had picked out the proper limousine and Cruz had fallen into casual conversation with the driver, laughing at some joke they shared before he whipped a fist into the chauffeur's stomach, cracked another hard against his jaw and dragged him toward the alleyway where Bolan waited, watching from the shadows.

The driver's uniform wasn't a perfect fit, but it would pass a casual inspection in the dark. The kind of folks who ride around in limousines aren't renowned for worrying what their chauffeur wears. Bolan's main concern, from

that point on, revolved around how many guests or bodyguards were with Ernesto Aguilar.

The restaurant was busy, and they had a while to wai
before the deputy minister of commerce and internal affair.
finished his meal. Bolan was used to waiting, but he fel
exposed, lounging beside Cruz in the limo's shotgun seat
pretending he belonged there. Still, the darkness and th
basic principle of role camouflage served him well. Late
diners passing by ignored him, presuming he was an em-
ployee of some bigger, better man inside the restaurant, and
never gave his Anglo face a second glance.

Cruz knew their target and spotted Aguilar the momen
he appeared. "That's him," he said, and pointed to a slender man attired in formal evening garb proceeding toward
the sidewalk with a younger woman hanging on his arm
There seemed to be no muscle trailing Aguilar. It was a
stroke of luck, if they could only keep his date from going
wild.

"Let's go."

Bolan slid off his seat and hunkered down below th
dash, knees pressed against his chest. There was more room
up front than in a normal car, but he could still feel muscles
cramping in his calves and thighs from the contortion necessary to conceal himself. The limo pulled a few yards
forward, and the dome lights flared as Cruz hopped out to
hold the door for Aguilar and his companion.

They were rolling in another moment, Bolan staying
where he was until they had completed several turns, putting the commercial district well behind them. Aguilar was
slow to notice, otherwise preoccupied. When Bolan eased
up and into view, he found the minister with one hand
halfway up the woman's thigh, beneath her skirt.

"Doors locked?" he asked Cruz.

"Yes," Cruz said, and pressed a button on the armrest

of his door, locking the limo. Again, the minister of commerce didn't notice as he focused on a very different goal.

Bolan was aiming the Beretta 93-R at them when he said, "Be careful of those fingers, *señorita*. There's no telling where they've been."

Two startled faces whipped around to gape at him, the minister retreating from his soft probe, while the woman gave a quick tug on her skirt. Bolan held the initiative, forging ahead before his prisoners could think of anything to say.

"Do you speak English, Mr. Aguilar?" he asked.

"English? Why...yes, I do," the minister replied.

"Good deal. Scoot up here, would you? I don't like to shout, and something tells me you don't want the lady hearing what I have to say."

Aguilar frowned, muttered something to the woman in Spanish, then made his way forward, one hand braced on the side wall to keep from pitching over on his face. He took a seat at point-blank range, eyes on the pistol. Bolan left it where it was, the muzzle angled into empty space between the minister and his companion.

"Who are you? What do you want?" he asked. A closer look at Cruz behind the wheel, and Aguilar was moved to add, "Where is Jaime?"

Assuming Jaime was the driver Cruz had KO'd, Bolan said, "He had to take a little nap. Our names are unimportant. What we want, however, could be vital if you want to stay alive."

"It's ransom, yes? You'll be disappointed, I'm afraid. My government will pay you nothing. It's the policy."

From Aguilar's expression and his tone, Bolan believed him. He had no doubt whatsoever that a deputy minister of this or that was considered expendable. Some other ambitious leech would always pay to get the job and line his pockets, dipping into public funds, concluding side deals with the predators he was supposed to keep at bay.

"Of course," the minister went on, "I have a little money of my own. Not much, you understand, but—"

"Keep your money," Bolan interrupted him. "It doesn't interest me."

"Oh, God." The hope went out of Aguilar on hearing that, as if someone had punctured his balloon and let the air escape. He slumped back in his seat and fumbled in his pockets for a handkerchief to wipe his face. "Oh, God," he said again. "Who sent you? Whose idea was this?"

"You've got the wrong idea," Bolan replied. "If all I wanted was to kill you, you'd be dead by now. And so would she."

"But you...you said..." The minister was flustered, visibly confused.

"I said we didn't want your money," Bolan said. "What we require from you is help with some negotiations we have underway."

"Negotiations?"

"You know Major Miguel Duende, with the state security police?"

The minister was frowning now. He said, "Of course I do."

"His goons picked up a woman earlier tonight. Her name is Ariana Vasquez. We're spreading the word that we want her released safe and sound, without further delay. Failure to comply has drastic consequences."

"But...but I'm not involved with the security police," said Aguilar.

"Oh, really? A deputy minister of the interior has no involvement with state security? That strikes me as peculiar," Bolan said.

"He's lying!" Cruz was glaring hard at Aguilar, his eyes reflected in the rearview mirror as he spoke.

"Well, I—"

"I guess you're not connected to the Triads, either," Bolan interrupted Aguilar again. "You have no piece of the narcotics traffic or the Chinese military crowd behind the Port Authority. We've got the wrong man, here," he said to Cruz. "This one's no use to us at all."

He thumbed back the Beretta's hammer, swung the muzzle with its custom sound suppressor to find a point between Ernesto Aguilar's bulging eyes. The minister gave a squeal of panic, lurched back in his seat and started babbling for dear life.

"No! Wait! I'll help you! I'll speak to Major Duende, certainly. If his men have this woman—"

"There's no 'if,'" Bolan informed him. "It's a fact."

"—and if she's still alive—"

"You'd better hope she is. You'd better pray. There's just no telling what may happen if she's not."

"I understand," the minister replied.

"I hope so. If she's dead, the town goes up in smoke, but you won't be around to see it burn. Understand?"

"Yes."

Cruz slowed the limousine, pulling it to the curb in a neighborhood of dark and silent shops. "Okay, we've got a deal, then," Bolan said. "Your life for hers. Now, take a hike."

The door locks clicked as Cruz reached out and thumbed the master button, Aguilar and his lady scrambled out of the limo before Bolan could change his mind.

"You think he'll talk to Duende?" Bolan asked, as Cruz drove on.

"No doubt," Cruz said. "I only wonder what he'll say."

"I guess we'd better shake a few more cages," Bolan told him, "just in case."

FELIZ RICCARDO loved his work. Three years before, he would have said it was disastrous when he found himself court-martialed and discharged from military service for the rape of several peasant women, mostly Indians. He wasn't sent to prison, granted, but the loss of status—not to mention steady paychecks and a pension, down the road—impressed Riccardo as a grave injustice. What had he done to deserve such persecution? Everybody knew the peasant women loved it. Who did his judges think they were deceiving with their pious words and attitudes, pretending they had never done the same or worse when they were common soldiers in the ranks?

It wasn't long, however, until young Feliz Riccardo realized that the army had done him a favor. He had been out of uniform for barely a month when he was approached by a recruiter for the death squads. They had checked his record, knew what he was made of, the kind of soldier he had been. It was apparent that he wouldn't flinch from dirty work, and when they tested him—picking a random target, so they said, and ordering Riccardo to eliminate the man— he had complied at once, no questions asked.

The rest, as someone said, was history. Feliz Riccardo was immune to further punishment by any organization of the state, his orders passed down from on high and secretly approved by those who mattered in the capital. These days, when he went hunting for subversives, criminals, the scum of so-called civilized society, he wasn't handcuffed by a book of rules dictating how he must conduct himself or treat his enemies. Those he was sent to punish had been tried, found guilty and the sentence had been death.

The best part, though, was that Riccardo got to have some fun along the way. He liked it best when he was sent to punish women and relished every sobbing plea for mercy, every scream.

Tonight, there had been trouble, but Feliz Riccardo wasn't frightened for himself. Some suicidal idiot had burned the headquarters of the Crusade for Public Decency, and there had been reported shooting incidents, mostly involving the Chinese. Feliz Riccardo personally didn't care if all of them were killed. Their fate was no concern of his. He had his orders to protect a storage complex on the north side of the city, where the death squad kept a stash of weapons, ammunition and assorted loot retrieved from liquidated targets.

Feliz Riccardo reckoned that he should be grateful for an easy job, watching the hoard and arsenal, instead of riding through the streets all night searching for gunmen. This way, he could relax, kick back, enjoy himself in peace and quiet.

He sat at one end of the gravel drive between two rows of storage cubicles, his metal folding chair leaning on two legs, with his shoulders pressed against the wall, his feet dangling free. The other men on duty with him had been stationed around the place, guarding six rows of storage sheds in all. Even sitting at a distance from the nearest floodlight to avoid the swirl of moths and other flapping insects, Riccardo still had ample light with which to read his magazine. Well, reading wasn't quite the proper term, since he was only checking out the pictures, graphic scenes of naked women, two and three together at a time, engaged in carnal pleasures that confirmed his view of females. All of them were sluts, regardless of their age, their race, their social standing. Some were better at concealing it than others, but a man who knew his business could—

The sudden clatter of an automatic weapon startled Feliz Riccardo, making him lose his balance and sending him tumbling sideways from his chair. Riccardo cursed as he made a lunge to grab the shotgun that was propped against the corrugated metal wall beside his chair.

More firing, and he heard a cry of pain from someone who had stopped a bullet, cut off suddenly as if by a descending ax. Riccardo grabbed the shotgun, a Benelli M-1 Super 90 semiautomatic with extended combat magazine, and struggled to his feet, cursing again as gravel tore his slacks and gouged his knees. Someone would pay for this!

He was advancing toward the sounds of gunfire when another battle was engaged somewhere behind him, instantly confusing him, dividing his attention. More than one attacker, then, which fit with the reports they had received. What solitary man would dare attack the death squads—or the Triads, for that matter—in the very capital itself? Some peasant rebel group, perhaps, or crazy bastards from the damned M-20 Group, who stubbornly refused to understand their day had passed.

Riccardo didn't really care who his opponents were, as long as he could find a way to take them by surprise, and preferably from behind. There was no shame in back-shooting. It did the job effectively and with a minimum of risk. Feliz Riccardo never faced an armed man if he could avoid it, preferring an ambush over a stand-up fight any day of the week.

Riccardo was deciding which way he should go, continue toward the street or turn and head the other way, when an explosion rocked the earth beneath his feet. He swiveled toward the sound, in time to see a fireball rising from the general direction of the rental office. Someone else was screaming now, as if in brutal pain, and once again the cries were silenced by a burst of automatic fire.

Feliz Riccardo had begun to think in terms of where to hide, instead of where to seek his enemies, but in another heartbeat he discovered that he had already wasted too much time. More thunderous explosions flung debris and smoke into the night. Riccardo tried to dodge, but he was struck by the shock wave of a blast no more than thirty feet behind him. The concussion swept him off his feet and punched him through a sloppy somersault. He landed on one shoulder and felt his collarbone implode. He squealed in pain as he flopped over on his back.

Did he lose consciousness? Riccardo couldn't say with any certainty. If so, he was awakened by the sound of crackling flames, the heat against his face and the pronouncement of an unfamiliar voice.

"We've got a live one over here," the stranger said in English.

Footsteps crunched on gravel, drawing closer, while Riccardo tried to find a weapon. He had lost the shotgun when he fell, but he still wore a pistol on his belt. Trying to reach it, he discovered that his right arm was disabled, no response to his commands beyond another flare of white-hot pain from his fractured clavicle. He tried the left arm, fumbling for a cross-hand draw, but then a shadow fell across his face and someone said, "That's not the best idea you ever had."

Riccardo blinked away his tears of pain and saw the muzzle of a submachine gun pointed at his face. The man behind it was a gringo, tall and grim. Another man stepped up beside him, this one Hispanic, carrying a weapon Riccardo recognized as an old Tommy gun.

"You've got one chance to walk away from this," the gringo said. "Well, maybe crawl away."

His sidekick had begun to translate when Riccardo said, "I speak English."

"Better yet." The gringo didn't seem to gloat. He simply didn't care about Feliz Riccardo, whether he survived or not. "You know a fellow named Quintana?"

This could be a trick, Riccardo knew. And yet, if they had found the storage sheds, defeated his companions with a swift surprise attack, it stood to reason that they knew about the death squad. What harm could it do to simply answer?

"*Sí,*" he told the gringo. "I mean, yes."

"We let you live, you take a message to him. Fair enough?"

"A message?" Sudden hope surged, a chance that he would actually survive.

"Quintana needs to call Miguel Duende of the state security police. Duende has a prisoner, a woman, who must be released. You understand?"

"A woman?" Riccardo was confused. "There will be many women prisoners."

"Duende knows the one we mean. That's not a problem. What Quintana needs to do is make that call. *Comprende?* While Duende holds the woman, nothing's sacred. No one's safe. Not your *compadres,* not the Triads. Nobody. You understand?"

"I'll tell him."

"See that you do."

And they were gone. It took a moment for Feliz Riccardo to decide that it wasn't a trick, they weren't standing back and waiting to assassinate him when he tried to crawl away. At last, when he had craned his head as far as possible and saw no evidence of living soul around him, he had struggled to his feet, tears streaming down his face and staggered farther from the spreading flames.

He needed medical attention, but the hospital would have to wait. First thing, Riccardo had to find a telephone and make that call.

MAJOR MIGUEL DUENDE had dismissed his aide after the fourth phone call, deciding it was best for him to take the rest himself. He had no doubt there would be more. Indeed, it seemed that half the fat cats in the city had decided they should call on him this night. Thus far, he had been contacted by David Ling on behalf of the Triads; by Adolfo Quintana, speaking for the death squads; by the Colombian maggot Jorge Rochon; and, most surprisingly, by no less than Ernesto Aguilar himself.

Their messages were all the same. Duende's soldiers had a woman in their custody, one Ariana Vasquez by name, whose immediate release was urgently desired by all concerned. A group of lunatics had run amok in the city, striking at selected targets, killing as they went, demanding freedom for the woman via dazed survivors at the scene of each attack. The men who telephoned Duende were convinced that more raids would ensue, with even greater loss of life and property, if he didn't comply with the demand.

As for the major, he was sorry that his men had picked the bitch up in the first place. What a stroke of foul luck that had been. Duende had interrogated her at length, with more than common zeal, until he was persuaded that she couldn't tell him where Guillermo Cruz or any other stray survivors of the rebel movement might be found. A wasted night, despite the pleasure he derived from touching her, watching her body twitch and writhe, hearing the music of her screams.

It was worse than a waste of time, in fact, for now he had all manner of unpleasantness to deal with. He wasn't concerned about Quintana's protest, though it troubled him to learn that members of the death squad had been killed, some of their valuable loot and arms destroyed. Quintana was Duende's creature and would ultimately do as he was told. The others...well, they were trouble.

He couldn't ignore the Triads or the damned Colombians while they were under the protection of his government, and that brought Duende back to his superior, Ernesto Aguilar. It would be child's play for a cabinet minister, even a deputy, to have Duende transferred, possibly demoted, maybe even dropped from the security police. He harbored an immense contempt for Aguilar, the politician who gave orders but preferred to keep his hands clean. Still, the major recognized his own place in the scheme of things and understood that there was nothing to be gained from futile gestures of defiance. If he got through this, survived the latest test intact, there would be time and opportunity to plot revenge on Aguilar. For now, Major Duende had to look out for himself.

He had a problem, though. The woman was alive, but rather badly injured. His enthusiasm had transformed into fury when he realized that she was useless to him, and while he wasn't particularly proud of his excess, it didn't trouble Duende in a moral sense. The difficulty was, simply stated: he couldn't release the woman to the streets, alone, unaided. If he simply had his soldiers dump her in a gutter somewhere, she would likely die before her friends arrived, and what would Duende gain from that except more grief?

The answer to his problem came by telephone, at 2:15 a.m. Major Duende let the phone ring twice before he lifted the receiver. He must not appear too desperate. It was a sign of weakness he couldn't abide.

"Hello?"

The caller spoke to him in Spanish. Duende didn't recognize the voice. There was no reason he should, though he couldn't help wondering if he was talking to Guillermo Cruz. But, then again, what difference did it make?

"Two questions, Major. Is the woman still alive?"

Duende didn't hesitate. "She is. May I inquire—"

"No. Second question—are you willing to release her?"

Hesitating now, as if he had to think it over, striving for some pretense of authority. "I see no reason why she should remain in custody," he said at last, sounding magnanimous. "She has responded adequately to our questions, and no charges have been filed."

The caller muttered something to himself, or possibly to someone else. Duende couldn't make it out, but he detected anger in the stranger's tone. "When will she be released?"

"There is, perhaps, one difficulty," Duende said. "The prisoner sustained some minor injuries while resisting arrest. She assaulted my officers, in fact, but since none of them was injured, we won't be pressing charges."

"How convenient for your officers."

Duende let the insult pass. "However," he continued, "it would probably be best if someone came to pick her up, you understand? She has no vehicle, and in her present state...well, we've received reports of violence around the city all night long and it would be uncivilized to let a woman walk the streets alone."

The caller's tone was stiff as he replied, "Perhaps we can arrange for a delivery on neutral ground."

Duende thought about that for a moment, smiling as he saw the glimmer of a plan. "An excellent idea," he said. There was no need to feign the pleasure that he felt. "If you will only tell me where and when...?"

It was the caller's turn to hesitate, some object covering the mouthpiece while the matter was discussed with others. Duende waited patiently, already savoring the grim solution to his difficulty.

"Very well," the caller said, back on the line. He gave directions to the drop. Duende memorized the place and smiled again. It was a perfect choice.

"One hour," he announced. "If that's satisfactory, of course."

"One hour, and no mistakes," the stranger said, then severed the connection.

Major Duende cradled the receiver, then immediately lifted it again. There were arrangements to be made, and he had no spare time to waste.

Quintana answered on the second ring, a muttered, *"Sí?"*

"Wake up, Adolfo," Duende said. "It's time for you to earn your daily bread."

10

When Ariana Vasquez woke the third or fourth time, realizing there would be no respite from her pain, she had lost track of time. She had no clock, no windows and her grip on consciousness was tenuous, at best. It slipped away from her like water dribbling through her fingers, and she had no way of knowing, when she came around, how much time had elapsed while she was out.

One thing was certain: she hadn't been moved.

The bunk on which she lay was still the same unyielding slab of metal, bolted to a cement wall. The threadbare blanket wrapped around her naked, aching body smelled of sweat and stale tobacco smoke. She would have tossed it from her, but the room was cold—or seemed that way to her, at least. She wondered if she was in shock, the chill a warning sign of vital systems making ready to shut down.

So be it. If she died, at least she had the satisfaction of resisting her tormentors to the bitter end. They hadn't managed to reveal the only secret she possessed, although their failure was as much a matter of coincidence as any great endurance on her part. The pain had broken her. She wouldn't deny that, even to herself. She would have told the major anything to stop it, but Duende's own deficiency had given her a method of resistance.

He had simply never asked about the gringo, seemed to have no clue that she and Cruz had gained a foreign ally in their fight, while Duende and his killers had been busy wiping out the mountain camp. He asked about Cruz time and time again, of course, along with others, some of whom were dead, some missing, and a handful Vasquez didn't know by name.

But he had missed the heart of it, and she could only hope the error would prove fatal for him, in the end. Vasquez herself wouldn't see it. She was as good as dead. If the interrogation didn't kill her from internal injuries or some bizarre infection, she would certainly be executed soon. A pistol bullet in the head was said to be traditional. The bastards called you out, pretending it was time to take a shower, maybe see a visitor, and when your back was turned—

She had begun to slip again, but she was startled back to full alertness by the scraping of a key inside the lock that kept her prisoner. The door to Vasquez's cell swung open and it took the last full measure of her courage to refrain from whimpering as Major Duende stepped into the cell. His uniform was freshly pressed, cap squarely seated on his head, and Vasquez thought he had to have shaved since she had seen him last. He smelled of something, but she couldn't say if it was alcohol or cheap cologne.

"Good news," he said, and Vasquez cringed inside, afraid of what would follow. Had they run Cruz down? Was Duende here to question her again? "You are to be released."

"Released?" Her own voice sounded hollow, far away. Was that some euphemism for the firing squad, perhaps? She knew Duende well enough to hate him, and to realize that nothing he might say was trustworthy. There had to be some trick behind his words, but she couldn't prevent herself from hoping that it might be true.

"Released," he said again, as if to reassure her. "You have friends outside who have negotiated for your freedom. They are most persuasive men."

"What friends?" she asked him, sitting up, the blanket pulled around her shoulders like a cape.

"It's not for me to say," the major answered. "I have orders to obey, like any other servant of the people. I am told, 'Release the Vasquez woman,' and I say farewell to you, although I have enjoyed our time together."

The bastard was mocking her. He was gloating even now.

"You'd send me out like this?" she asked, and shrugged inside the blanket, just enough to make it move a little, without setting off new flares of pain.

"By no means, Ariana." As he spoke, the major snapped his fingers and a twenty-something soldier wearing sergeant's stripes entered the cell, a paper shopping bag supported in both hands. At Duende's signal he approached the cot and set the bag beside her then reversed direction through the open door and disappeared.

"Your clothes," Duende said. "Get dressed and I'll return for you in, say, ten minutes. Don't delay. We have no time to waste."

Duende stepped outside and left the door ajar. She wondered if he might be watching her, but then again what difference could it make? She had no secrets from the major where her body was concerned. She was beyond embarrassment, humiliation, even shame.

But she wasn't beyond the pain.

It hurt like blazes, pulling on her slacks and blouse, bending to tie her shoes, but Vasquez somehow got it done with time to spare. She counted off a full three minutes in her head before Duende reappeared.

"All ready? Excellent," he said, beaming another hungry smile. "If you'll come along...."

"Where are you taking me?" she asked, almost past caring if she lived or died, but still not trusting him.

"A meeting's been arranged with your friends," Duende

said. "You'll be delivered there in roughly half an hour. Come, now! There's a schedule to be kept."

The sharp tone of his voice was more familiar, and it made her cringe a little, but she still found strength to stand and cross the room. Duende stood to the side to let her pass in front of him, directing her along a narrow hallway. She passed more doors like hers and wondered who was locked away behind them, saddened to discover that she really didn't care. As long as she got out, what difference did it make? She couldn't save the world.

And, at the moment, Ariana Vasquez wasn't even certain she could save herself.

QUINTANA STOOD before two dozen of his best men and scanned their faces, making note of scowls and scars, an eye patch here, a birthmark there. Most of them wouldn't pass for handsome; two or three of them were downright hideous. If he had been recruiting models for a fashion magazine, that would have been a problem. As it was, he simply needed stone-cold killers who could do the job assigned to them, efficiently, without remorse.

There were no questions when he finished the briefing. That was as it should be, since the plan was rudimentary. An idiot could pull it off, providing he had nerve enough to kill and not run off like some pathetic coward the first time one of his opponents fired a shot.

These men were all ex-soldiers, ex-policemen, with three or four contract assassins thrown into the mix. Between them, these two dozen shooters probably had killed five hundred men, perhaps a great deal more. The former cops and military men among them had been exiled from the service on disciplinary charges, most of them involving acts of violence that exceeded their authority.

"You understand what must be done?" Quintana asked the group. Some of them nodded, others muttered in reply.

A couple of them shrugged, but he ignored them, knowing they weren't as stupid as they looked.

"You'll proceed immediately to the waterfront," he told them. "Vehicles are waiting for you on the street. Remember not to fire on the officers who drop the woman off."

A couple of his soldiers started snickering at that, but stopped immediately when Quintana pinned them with a glare. These men, for all their training, all the blood that they had spilled, knew better than to test his patience on important matters. He was worse than any of them, and had proved it frequently enough that only those with suicidal tendencies would think of crossing him.

"Go, now!" Quintana snapped, and watched them file out through the exit. The gunners left an odor in their wake, two parts testosterone, one part gun oil, and one part perspiration. They were no sooner out of sight, than he began to question whether they could do the job.

Quintana's problem, simply stated, was that he had no idea who they were up against, how many adversaries they would have to face, what kinds of weapons were available to soldiers of the other side. The bastards had incendiaries, that much he could state with certainty, from the destruction of CPD headquarters and, more recently, the storage facility where much of his own arsenal had been stashed. They had at least one skillful sniper, based on the complaints from Colonel Bao Bai-fan and Lin Shao-pei—though why the two Chinese hadn't been killed was still a mystery Quintana couldn't penetrate. One of his own surviving soldiers had described two gunmen, one of them a gringo, and that report squared with the babbling of Jorge Rochon, though neither man could swear the two he saw were unaccompanied by other gunmen.

Quintana told himself that he shouldn't be worried. He had sent two dozen of his toughest men to do a job that called for half that number, maybe less. If only two men really were responsible for the attacks this night, his troops would have them comfortably outnumbered, twelve to one. In any case, his soldiers knew the waterfront, they were cold-blooded killers and they feared his wrath above all else.

What could go wrong?

The very notion made the leader of the death squads smile.

"THEY WILL be waiting for us, yes?"

"Most definitely, yes," Bolan replied. He was relieved to see that Cruz didn't appear discouraged by the thought. Cruz had finished cleaning his Thompson, reloading two spent magazines and double-checking the 50-round drum. Now he was working on the Walther semiauto pistol, leaving nothing to chance.

"Do you think Ariana is alive?" Cruz asked.

It was the question that had preyed on Bolan's mind, and he could see that it weighed more heavily on Cruz, with his obvious affection for the woman. Whether Cruz had ever dared to voice his feelings, Bolan didn't know, but he had no doubt that Cruz was prepared to die for her, if it came to that.

"I can't be sure," he told Cruz, honestly, "but I believe she is. If nothing else, Duende knows that he may have to show her off at the delivery, to draw us out and let his gunners have a shot. He couldn't do that with a corpse. It's easier to bring her in alive, and shoot her when they open up on us."

Cruz's teeth were clenched when he replied, "We must be swift and sure, then. I don't want Ariana harmed."

There was no need to state the obvious. He had relayed Duende's vague remarks about the minor injuries Vasquez had suffered while resisting arrest, and Cruz, of all people, knew what to expect when a rebel was held for interrogation by the state security police. The injuries could amount to anything from scrapes and bruises to electric shock, gang rape or broken bones. They wouldn't know until they had retrieved the woman from Duende's custody, and even then, she might not be inclined to share the details with another living soul.

Whatever Vasquez might have suffered in the clutches of their common enemy, it was her cross to bear, her story to share or withhold as she chose. He wouldn't ask and neither would Guillermo Cruz if he was wise. That sharing came with trust and time.

Vengeance, meanwhile, wasn't required to wait so long. Bolan completed his survey of chosen hardware for the mission. In addition to the Spectre submachine gun, he was carrying a Steyr AUG assault rifle. The 5.56 mm bullpup design manufactured in Austria was widely adopted by armies and law enforcement agencies around the world for its accuracy and dependability in adverse combat conditions. At thirty-one inches overall, the AUG was three inches shorter than the smallest model of the M-16 and offered more reliable firepower, plus the added benefit of its untraceability to the United States. Bolan's traditional side arms topped off the killer ensemble, with an assortment of smoke and antipersonnel grenades.

Whatever happened on the waterfront this night, he meant to be prepared.

The plan was basic: they would roll into the meet ahead of time and hope the opposition wasn't there before them. They would stake out the drop zone, chart fields of fire and prepare themselves—as much as possible—for whatever happened next.

"We'd better go," he told Cruz, packing his hardware into the OD duffel bag, adding the bandolier of spare magazines he would wear when the battle was joined.

"I'm ready," Cruz replied, snapping the 50-round

"gangster" drum into place on his Thompson, wrapping the weapon in a raincoat that carried his spare magazines in side pockets. It was still warm out, and muggy. Cruz could slip the coat on when they reached their destination. Meanwhile, his pistol was well hidden by the loose tail of his black knit shirt.

They took the same car they had used throughout the evening, though it wore new license plates from Cruz's emergency stash. Cruz drove, watching his speed and dutifully observing traffic signals on the way. Bolan could smell the waterfront before they got there, a perfume of brine, dead fish and diesel fuel.

From where he sat, it smelled like death.

"MY PLAN will work," Major Duende said. "I promise you!"

"I'm not concerned with promises," Ernesto Aguilar replied. "I want results. These bastards threatened me with guns, you understand? They kidnapped me and left my driver naked in a stinking alley with the rats. That such a thing could happen in the city is a shame and a disgrace. It makes me wonder if I shouldn't look for someone else to keep the peace."

It was a treat to watch Duende squirm, much better than insulting him by telephone, where Aguilar couldn't observe his groveling firsthand. That the mighty warrior, with so many polished medals on his chest, could be so easily emasculated by a few choice words made Aguilar feel better, let a tiny measure of his rage slip from him like evaporating sweat.

"I can assure you, Minister—"

"You have assured me, Major, time and time again, that you were in control of this distressing situation. When our Chinese friends were under fire in the Serrania del Darién, you came here and assured me that the problem had been solved, the bandits neutralized. Apparently, you were mistaken. They had merely shifted operations to the capital itself. You next assured me that their back was broken when you razed their camp above San Carlos. Once again, it seems that you were wrong. Since then, they have run rampant in the city while you dally with some peasant bitch who tells you nothing. Her arrest, meanwhile, provokes this scum to kidnap me and use me as an errand boy to pass along their ultimatums. That summarized your control and progress, doesn't it?''

''I wouldn't say—'' Duende saw the look that Aguilar was giving him and caught himself before he made another grievous error. Clearing his throat, he began anew. ''Yes, Minister. You are correct. As always.''

''Now, you have a brilliant plan to trap these rebels with the very woman whose arrest incited them to threaten me with death,'' said Aguilar. ''Will you be using members of the state security police for this assignment, Major?''

''No, sir,'' Duende said. ''I have arranged for…um, that is to say…for private contractors to deal with these subversives. They are very skilled, I promise you.''

''Of course,'' said Aguilar. ''We've seen their work before. And should they fail for any reason, you'll be spared the shame of having dead policemen scattered all around the waterfront.''

''It seems impossible that they will fail, *Jefé*,'' the major said.

''It seemed impossible to me that anyone would commandeer my limousine in the heart of Panama City,'' Aguilar retorted. ''And yet, it happened all the same. I find my tolerance for failure growing smaller by the hour, Miguel.''

Major Duende blinked at Aguilar's use of his given name, interpreting the intimacy as a warning. He was perfectly correct in that respect. Ernesto Aguilar had already decided to replace Duende if the current problem wasn't solved, and swiftly. There was far too much at stake for any motley band of peasants to derail the grand design.

A band of peasants. Suddenly, he had another thought. "About this gringo," Aguilar inquired. "Have you identified him, yet?"

"No, Minister." Duende's cheeks were darkly mottled with embarrassment. "We think he's a mercenary, but we can't be positive. There's no reason to believe that the Americans are aiding these subversives in their scheme."

"No reason that you know of," Aguilar corrected him.

"That is correct, *Jefé*. If you have any knowledge of such operations by the Yankees, I certainly appreciate the information," Duende said.

"And you would have it, Major. Obviously, I don't receive strategic briefings from the CIA or drug enforcement agents. I haven't been favored with reports from Washington. It is your job, as the commander of the state security police, to ferret out such operations and expose them. Is that not correct?"

"Yes, Minister." Duende's anger was already shifting back into humiliation.

"And when you had this peasant woman, when you questioned her, what did she say about the gringo? Did she know his name?"

Duende's eyes were blinking rapidly, as if synapses in his brain had started to misfire. "The gringo? Well...that is to say..."

"You did inquire about the Yankee, did you not, Miguel? It seems a rather basic question, under the circumstances."

"I did, of course," Duende answered, obviously lying through his yellow teeth. "The woman didn't know him."

"That's a pity, don't you think? If she had simply told you where to find this gringo, even named him, you could easily have captured him, no doubt. Our problem would be solved and we might even have a case against the arrogant Americans, something for the United Nations and the press to talk about. How sad she didn't know the man.''

"Indeed, *Jefé*," Duende said. "It would have made things so much simpler."

"Yes. But now you must achieve by force of arms what hasn't been accomplished by persuasion. I hope your 'independent contractors' are equal to the task, Miguel.''

"They have my utmost confidence," Duende told him.

"As they should," said Aguilar, "considering the fact that they are now responsible for your career.''

Duende stiffened, but at least he managed to control his eyelids. Finally, when he could trust his voice, the major said, "I understand.''

"I'm sure you do," the minister replied. "We're engaged in business dealings that will change the course of history for Panama, Major Duende. Nothing—no one— who obstructs that long-awaited progress will be tolerated. Those who falter in their duty or attempt to undermine our nation's future simply won't survive.''

"No, sir." The major's voice had dwindled to a whisper, though he kept his military bearing, sitting ramrod straight.

"You're excused, Major. I know you have important business to conduct, soldiers to supervise. The next time that we speak, I will expect good news.''

"And you shall have it, Minister.''

Aigular watched him leave and thought, I'll have it, or I'll have your head, you bastard.

Aguilar was only certain of one thing: whatever happened in the next few hours, if he went down, he wouldn't go alone.

11

Bolan took full advantage of the shadows as he waited for the enemy to show and drop off Ariana Vasquez. He didn't expect the handoff to go smoothly. On the contrary, Cruz had confirmed with his connection at the state security police that there would be a trap in place. A pair of uniforms would make the drop, backed by shooters from the death squad, their numbers, armament, and exact deployment unknown. It was enough for Bolan. He knew that when the shooting started, he could fight back without worrying about his adversaries.

The key point, still, was to prevent any further harm from befalling Ariana Vasquez. She had suffered enough—and Bolan had no doubt that she had suffered plenty—at the hands of the security police. Bolan surmised that she was meant to die in the exchange of gunfire on the waterfront, and while he wasn't certain he could save her, he would give it everything he had.

Upon arriving at the scene, he had a range of vantage points to choose from, but the two that seemed most useful were a tugboat moored against the pier and the roof of a defunct seafood restaurant, its windows boarded over. He flipped a mental coin and took the boat, preferring mobility over altitude this time, and Cruz had gone for the roof, uncovering a metal folding ladder in a nearby alleyway, pulling it up after him once he was in place.

Crouched in the stern of the tugboat, Bolan had a fair

amount of cover, both from casual passersby—none so far—and from incoming fire. It was a short, if somewhat awkward, hop from where he was onto the pier and then a quick sprint to the cover of a bait shack built from corrugated steel. Beyond that, any moves he made would depend on where his enemies were stationed and how many of them were arrayed against him. Cruz, on the high ground, could cover Bolan's movements if he had to, or engage whatever targets he could pick out from the roof. The Tommy gun's effective range was said to be 150 yards, but it would take an expert marksman and a miracle to score a hit with any submachine gun at that range. In this set, Cruz wouldn't be called upon to fire on any target farther than two hundred feet away, and that was pushing it. The good news: anyone he hit with the Thompson's heavy .45-caliber rounds was going to be in a world of hurt.

Bolan made a last-minute check of his hardware, patting the bandolier and making sure that he could find the hand grenades suspended from his combat webbing by touch. The Spectre SMG was strapped across his back on a quick-release sling, no wrenching and tugging over his head if he got in a tight spot. He held the Steyr AUG, a live round in the chamber and the safety off, its fire selector set for 3-round automatic bursts. The transparent plastic magazine in place held forty-two 5.56 mm rounds. The backups in his bandolier held thirty rounds a piece.

And if I need all that, the Executioner reminded himself, *I'm screwed.*

Waiting could be the worst of it, but Bolan was accustomed to the lull before the killing storm. It was a talent he had picked up as a Special Forces sniper in a very different war, and it had served him well since then. There was no trick to it. He simply waited, often motionless, sometimes for hours—even days—on end. He had learned to ignore heat and cold, biting insects, all manner of personal discomfort, to hold his place and make the killing shot. Bolan had been there countless times, before.

And still, he felt the sweet rush of adrenaline as headlights flared in front of him, a hundred yards downrange. They turned in his direction, a patrol car moving slowly down the road that ran along the waterfront. He raised the AUG, peered through the rifle's optical sight at the advancing vehicle.

And waited.

ARIANA VASQUEZ sat in the back of the patrol car in a cage of wire and glass. She wore handcuffs, a long chain fastening her manacles to a steel bar welded to the floorboard of the car beneath her feet. It had occurred to her that if they had an accident, if anything at all should happen to the car, she would be trapped inside. It seemed unlikely, granted, but her mind picked at the problem anyway. She couldn't bear the thought of suffering so much, coming so close to release and having freedom snatched away from her.

While those thoughts percolated in one corner of her brain, another part was telling Vasquez that her captors never meant to set her free at all. This was a trick, the small voice told her, sounding very like her own. Major Duende had some kind of game in mind, a trap to snare anyone who came to fetch her from captivity.

But who was left? A scattered handful, most of whom she barely knew by sight, much less by name. No, she decided. If anyone was waiting for her, it would be Guillermo Cruz and Mike Belasko. Duende's trick, his trap, would be for them.

They had been raising hell around the city when she was arrested. Vasquez didn't know what had been going on since then, but she had picked up bits and pieces from the officers assigned as her escorts. They kept their voices down, but she could still hear some of what they said. If she interpreted their cryptic words correctly, someone had demanded her release, compelled Major Duende to deliver her by lashing out at varied targets in a reign of terror. The policemen muttering in front of her were visibly intimidated, though they struck a macho pose for one another, both pretending they would like to face the men responsible and kill them, if they were only given half a chance.

Perhaps they meant it. Vasquez couldn't tell for sure. She did know that the young men had a rude surprise in store for them when they met Mike Belasko in the flesh.

Major Duende hadn't told her where she would be taken, and her escorts—while they obviously knew—wouldn't respond to any questions Vasquez asked them. After two attempts she had lapsed into silence, following their progress through the windows, watching out for landmarks as they drove along. It took some time for her to orient herself, and when she realized that they were heading for the docks, they were already halfway there.

What did it mean? Would they arrive to find a boat waiting, Cruz and the Yankee on board? It seemed unlikely, and she knew that an effort to escape by sea was easily defeated when the enemy had powerboats and helicopters standing by. They would be blown out of the water, sunk and drowned, before they could proceed a mile from shore.

And if they managed to escape, what then? Belasko could go back to the United States, but her home was here, in Panama. She didn't want to leave, become an exile from her own homeland, although she hated what was happening and what her nation had become. Still, she could never hope to change things from another country, hiding like a fugitive, afraid to show her face.

She felt a tide of bitter laughter welling up inside her, as she thought of hope and change. What hope? What change? This night's experience had taught her what could happen to the innocent in Panama, in case she needed a reminder. She would bear the marks throughout her life, if not on flesh, then on her soul. Why should she even try to change this country that had nearly killed her? Why attempt to help the thousands who accepted their pathetic lot in life as if they were so many sheep?

Before she had a chance to sort it out, deal with her bitterness, they reached the waterfront. The squad car slowed, making a left turn toward the docks, the headlights flicking onto high beams as the driver hit a switch. The lights swept over the facades of small-time businesses, all closed down for the night.

The driver stepped on the brake and brought the cruiser to a halt. He left the motor running with the headlights on, but shifted into neutral and set the parking brake. "I don't see anyone," he said at last.

"What difference does it make?" the other asked, checking his watch. "We're right on time. We drop her off and leave, that's all. It doesn't matter if they're here or not. Her problem if they don't show up."

The second officer was first to step out of the car; the driver following a moment later. Number two opened the door on Vasquez's right and reached in to unlock her handcuffs, then stepped back to let her exit. By the time she joined him on the pavement, he was standing with his pistol drawn, the weapon held against his thigh.

She had a momentary flash of panic, fearing he would shoot her now, but he made no attempt to raise the pistol. He clasped her arm with his free hand and guided her toward the front of the patrol car, the path illuminated by its headlights. The officers fell into step behind her, side by side, their very presence urging her along.

When she had covered twenty paces and the car was well behind her, Vasquez hesitated, turning back to face the two policemen, still expecting trickery. The driver made a shooing motion with his hand. "Go on," he said. "Get out of here."

And then his head exploded like a ripe tomato crushed beneath a hammer. Vasquez heard the shot a heartbeat later, already recoiling from the sight, aware of warm blood spattered on her face and shirt. The scream she tried to utter came out sounding like a strangled hiss.

She turned and fled into the darkness, running for her life.

GUILLERMO CRUZ was covering the two policemen while watching for other adversaries lurking in the shadows when the shot rang out. It startled him, and as he saw the first cop fall, he wondered what had made the American change his mind about shooting policemen. Then, before that thought was fully formed, Cruz realized the gunshot's sound was wrong, too loud and deep to issue from the gringo's automatic rifle.

In the time it took for Cruz to work that out—a second, maybe two—a firestorm broke across the waterfront. The second officer already had his pistol drawn, and now, instead of looking for the gunman who had killed his partner, he took aim at Vasquez. The muzzle-flash and sharp report shook Cruz out of his brief paralysis and brought the heavy Thompson into target acquisition.

The gringo might have scruples about shooting members of the state security police, but Cruz had no such mental handicap. He framed the slender figure in his sights, flinched as a second pistol shot rang out, then triggered off a burst that dropped the shooter where he stood, leaving deep crimson splashed across his khaki uniform.

Guns seemed to open up from everywhere at once, their muzzle-flashes winking up and down the waterfront like fireflies in the early morning darkness. Cruz knew where Bolan was aboard the tug, which meant the rest of these were enemies, all bent on killing him, killing the gringo, killing Vasquez.

Christ, so many! He hadn't imagined they would send so many gunners to the waterfront, but it was clear Duende meant to finish it right here, right now. Cruz hoped that he could disappoint the major. Failing that, he meant to take a few more of the bastards with him on his way to Hell.

The Thompson had a fair kick to it, and the muzzle liked to climb. Cruz fought it, thankful he had reattached the wooden shoulder stock. He sighted on the muzzle-flashes of his nearest enemies and fired short bursts, ducking when they responded and their bullets swarmed around him like mosquitoes in the night. He had no body armor. It would only take one hit to put him down, but he was focused on the threat to Vasquez, desperate to cover her retreat.

It might already be too late, of course—the first or second shot from the policeman could have struck her—but Cruz wouldn't let himself believe that. He had seen her running, knew she was alive short moments earlier, and that was how he would imagine her until he saw the body for himself.

Assuming he survived that long.

Two of his enemies had gained the rooftop of the shop next door to Cruz's perch. They were advancing on him now, both firing from the hip with automatic weapons, bullets snapping through the air around him, one round tugging at his sleeve. Cruz spun to face them, leveling the Thompson, holding down the trigger as the walking shadows lurched into his sights.

Cruz saw his targets twitching, jerking, and he took a brief, fierce satisfaction from their screams as they went down. He didn't know if they were dead or merely wounded, but they had been neutralized for now, unlike the other gunmen who were pouring automatic fire toward his position, tearing up the roof around him, ripping great holes in the air-conditioning compressor where he crouched to shield himself.

Where was Belasko? Was the gringo even still alive?

It made no difference. There was a battle to be fought, and Cruz was in it to the death. He wished the American well and prayed Vasquez might have found a place to hide. Then he came out firing, answering the hostile automatics burst for burst.

BOLAN HAD NO idea why any member of the death squad hunting party would have opened fire on Vasquez's escorts, and he had no time to think about it once the battle had been joined. The first cop had been cut down by a sniper, while the second, firing after Vasquez, had been snuffed by Cruz's Tommy gun. All hell broke loose at that point and Bolan lost track of Vasquez as she vanished in the shadows, away to his left. The squad car was taking hits, but most of the incoming fire was directed at Guillermo Cruz on the roof of the restaurant across from Bolan. Cruz had revealed himself with his short burst of automatic fire, and the death squad gunners were doing their best to topple him from his perch.

The Executioner started tracking with the AUG, framing muzzle-flashes in the Steyr's optical sight, then adjusting to find the man behind the gun before he sent 3-round bursts crackling into the darkness. He saw one shadow slump, its weapon silenced, followed quickly by a second and a third. The shooters had his range by then, and bullets started rattling off the tugboat's hull, smashing out the cabin windows above and behind him. Tough luck for the owner when he showed up the next day. Bolan hoped his boat was insured.

The Executioner nailed two more of his adversaries, saw a couple of them dropped by Cruz's Tommy gun, before he heard a soft, familiar-sounding *pop* amidst the general din. His mind made the connection just in time for Bolan to vault the tug's stern rail, sprawling on the dock facedown, a heartbeat before the 40 mm high-explosive grenade came in on target, detonating on impact with the tugboat's cabin.

The blast showered Bolan with shards of debris, driving spikes of pain into his ears, but it also covered his escape with a sudden swirl of smoke. The tug was burning and Bolan made it to the nearby bait shed just before the diesel tanks erupted in a fiery secondary blast.

A cheer went up from someone on the opposition team, but most were still pouring fire at Cruz. Bolan resumed his task of sniping at them with short, precision bursts, and in another moment the survivors realized they had more trouble on their hands. By that time, based on a rapid count of muzzle-flashes, he and Cruz had trimmed their numbers by half, at least.

And it was time to move again, before they pinned him down. Bolan broke from cover, running in a zigzag pattern, bullets snapping at his heels. He reached the doorway of a darkened shop and stayed their long enough to palm a smoke grenade, release the pin and lob it into the middle of the frontage road. While he was waiting for the smoke to spread, he loosed a frag grenade and primed it, standing ready with the AUG in one hand, grenade in the other, counting down the seconds until it was time to make his move.

He came out firing from the hip, Cruz helping with a long burst from the rooftop, spilling an unwary death squad sniper to the pavement down below. A couple more were sheltered in the alleyway behind another shop ahead of Bolan and he pinned them down with automatic fire until he had a chance to toss the frag grenade. Its smoky thunderclap propelled one twisted body out into the street, the other smeared on walls and gravel.

Bolan charged. In other circumstances, it wouldn't have been his chosen strategy, but they were running out of time. The racket, even in a more-or-less deserted neighborhood like this, would certainly result in calls to the police, and if Duende didn't send reinforcements, someone farther down the food chain might just beat him to it. Someone in the dark about the major's plan, perhaps, who still thought the police were meant to fight crime, rather than committing it.

And so, he rushed ahead, Cruz keeping pace with him across the rooftops. They hosed the night with automatic fire, targeting muzzle-flashes, startled voices, moving shadows in the greater darkness. When the Steyr's magazine ran out, Bolan let the rifle dangle from its shoulder strap, unhooked the Spectre SMG and kept firing, lobbing more grenades to punctuate the spray of death. And when the Spectre's fifty rounds were spent, he drew his side arms, the Beretta 93-R stuttering in 3-round bursts, the heavy Desert Eagle thundering at targets who recoiled from the sledgehammer blows.

It was impossible to mark the instant when the firefight ended. Gunfire rang in Bolan's ears for moments afterward, but there were no more bullets singing through the air around him, no more dodging, cursing targets anywhere in sight. He stepped into the middle of the frontage road and drew no hostile fire, looked up and found Cruz watching him, a tight smile on his face, the Thompson smoking in his hands.

And it was finished, just like that.

Almost.

Cruz found a fire escape and scrambled down to street level. They were retreating toward the car and watching out for Vasquez, when she stepped into the street. Incredibly, one of the squad car's headlights was still burning, though the engine had been put to sleep by gunfire. There was still juice in the battery, and in the cyclop's glare they saw her, one hand raised to shield her eyes against the light.

Cruz ran to her and swept her up into his arms, releasing her at once and muttering apologies when she cried out in pain. The two of them were whispering in Spanish, heads together, when the Executioner caught up. He saw the purple bruises marking Vasquez's face, but there was also something in her eyes, a gleam of something—hope? affection?—that evoked an unaccustomed smile from Cruz.

"Cops are coming," Bolan said, as distant sirens took the place of gunfire echoes.

"Let's go," Cruz said. He started to reach for Vasquez, hesitated and was satisfied to take her by the hand.

This part was finished, but the battle wasn't over yet by any means. His enemies were wounded, but they still had enough strength to fight, perhaps to win. The Executioner had plans for Panama and he would have to see them through before another day was out, or he might lose the opportunity forever.

Falling into step behind the would-be lovers, Bolan wondered if they would survive, if their newfound emotions would endure the trials that lay ahead. He wished them well and knew that part of it, at least, wasn't his call.

No one had ever mistaken Mack Bolan for Cupid.

Tonight, he was standing in for the Angel of Death.

12

In mortal combat, there was no such thing as standing still. Even defensive action in a fixed position still required some measure of mobility, if only on the part of individual combatants. Bolan, for his part, preferred to fight offensive actions that demanded ample combat stretch.

The safe apartment he had never used was waiting when they dropped off Vasquez, Cruz arranging for a doctor he could trust to make a house call and attend her wounds. There was no question of a hospital, and even calling in the friendly medic was a gamble, but Cruz wouldn't leave the woman without making some provision for her care. His face was carved as if in stone when he and Bolan left the flat and walked back to their latest set of wheels.

"What now?" Cruz asked.

"We finish what we started," Bolan told him, "turning them against each other. Since they didn't take the hint last time, we'll need to be a bit more obvious."

"So, what's our first stop?" Cruz inquired.

"Let's do the Triads," Bolan said. "We'll need to leave a witness, let him hear some Spanish. We can put on ski masks, if you want, but I don't think it makes much difference. Everybody knows all round-eyes look alike."

One of the targets still remaining on his hit list was an old downtown hotel that had been purchased by the Panama Port Authority two years earlier. Minimal renovations allowed the new owners to reopen, and the hotel had reached full capacity within days, its rooms sold out to a party of Chinese businessmen who were, in fact, soldiers for the Triad. Bolan guessed that some of them—perhaps a majority—would be out on patrol at that hour, if they weren't already casualties, but there were bound to be some gunners still in residence, winding down between shifts. He didn't need an army, after all—just a few bodies for show and tell.

And one witness.

They parked in back in another filthy alley that resembled all the others he had seen of late. Trash collection clearly didn't rank high on the list of civic priorities in Panama City, and the stench from nearby Dumpsters hit him like a slap across the face as Bolan stepped out of the car.

No problem. It would be worse yet, before they left.

They found the back door locked, and Bolan took a chance, two quick, sound-suppressed rounds from the Beretta 93-R, while Cruz stood ready with his Thompson, just in case their entry prompted an armed response. In fact, there was nothing, and they entered to the sound of blaring music that echoed from the floors above.

Four floors in all, with ten rooms each. In other circumstances, Bolan would have started at the top and worked his way down to the street, eliminating anyone he met along the way. This morning, though, he hadn't checked ahead to see how many gunners were in residence, and they were running short of time. More to the point, he didn't wish to fight a pitched, decisive battle with the Triads here and now when he would need a show of strength from their contingent later to complete his master plan.

"We're heading for the second floor," he told Guillermo Cruz. "Remember, there'll be more upstairs, so watch your back. And let them hear you."

"*Sí*, señor," Cruz said, and flashed a grin as hard and

bright as polished steel. His hatred for the enemy was palpable, and Bolan hoped it wouldn't get him killed.

They took the elevator, gambling, shaving seconds off their travel time. Emerging on the second floor, they met a pair of Triad gunners standing in the hallway, both with beer bottles in hand, one with a semiauto pistol showing in his belt. Before he had a chance to reach it, Bolan milked a short burst from his Spectre SMG and dropped them where they stood, beer mingling with the blood from tidy wounds.

The sound of gunfire brought more Triad members spilling out of rooms to left and right. Behind them, meanwhile, Bolan heard the elevator door slide shut, thus closing one path of retreat. He turned left toward the stairs and opened up on his surprised opponents, strafing them with hot 9 mm Parabellum rounds. Behind him, Cruz was blasting with the Thompson, ranting at his enemies in Spanish. Bolan couldn't follow most of it, but what he did make out was heavy on profanity and insults.

Moving toward the stairs, sidestepping bodies as he went, Bolan reached underneath his jacket and retrieved a frag grenade, released the pin and pitched it toward the stairwell. He watched it bounce once on the threadbare carpeting before it disappeared. The blast, five seconds later, was a clap of bottled thunder mixed with human screams.

He reached the stairs and started down, stepping over more bodies with Cruz behind him, still giving the Triads hell with his tongue and his Thompson. One of the guys at the base of the stairs was still moving, and Bolan kicked his gun away, leaning down to smack him in the face with the Spectre's smoking muzzle. Dazed but conscious, the Triad gunner watched them go.

More guns were waiting for them in the lobby, crouched behind the bargain-basement furniture. A second hand grenade dispersed them, scattering the shooters who could still get up and run or hobble for their lives. Wild shots knocked divots in the walls and ceiling, chewed a ragged zigzag path across the registration counter and raised a cloud of snow-white stuffing from a sofa in the middle of the room.

The Triad fighters were still pumping rounds at shadows in the smoky lobby, while their enemies slipped out the back. Bolan and Cruz were half a block away before the gunners spilled into the alley, with a futile burst of parting shots.

So far, so good, thought Bolan.

But the worst was yet to come.

DAVID LING had never been a patient man. It was a failing he had tried to overcome, without success. The pleasures of delayed gratification were lost on him, a foolish waste of precious time. He hated waiting, most particularly waiting for another person, and that well-known trait was sometimes used against him as a form of petty punishment, by the handful of people who could still pull rank on him, despite his status in the Triad.

One such person, the most galling of the lot, was Colonel Bao Bai-fan. Ling would never forgive the Beijing Communists for their harassment of the Triads, even when new bargains with the state contrived to make him wealthier, as in the case of Panama. The colonel was a living, breathing symbol of the system he despised, the Red disease personified, and it infuriated Ling to find himself at Bao's beck and call. This morning it was worse than ever, since he had more soldiers dead and couldn't move against the men responsible without approval from Beijing's man on the scene.

Ling had been sitting in the colonel's anteroom for fifteen minutes, feeling every second as it ticked away, his anger mounting as he sat and wasted time. It was preposterous that he should need a clearance from Beijing in order to defend himself, and yet...

A butler came to summon Ling. Finally.

The colonel's private office wasn't large, nor were the furnishings luxurious. Ling wondered whether Bao was so committed to the "people's revolution" that he favored Spartan styles, or if he had some treasure squirreled away, in case he someday had to flee.

"You've had some difficulty, David?" After wasting so much time, at least the colonel felt no need to dawdle with preliminary small talk.

"I have lost more soldiers," Ling informed him. "Thirteen dead and seven wounded. Two or three of those will also die, I think."

"That is unfortunate," the colonel said. His face showed no emotion whatsoever.

"It's a consequence of our peculiar business here," Ling answered. "I believe it was preventable. It certainly must be avenged."

"In order to avenge, you must identify the men responsible," Bao said.

"I know the men responsible," Ling said.

The colonel cocked an eyebrow. "Ah. By all means, let me have their names."

"They did not leave a business card behind," Ling sneered.

"In which case—"

"They were Panamanian! What else is there to know?"

The colonel frowned. "A great deal, it would seem. You surely don't suppose that everyone in Panama who owns a firearm also shares the same opinion of our enterprise?"

"These men weren't some peasant rabble," Ling retorted. "They were soldiers, trained in military tactics, armed with military weapons and grenades."

"Which tells you...what, exactly?" Colonel Bao inquired.

"It tells me that the people we do business with aren't

our friends,'' Ling answered. ''I have never trusted them. They look at us as if we smelled of rotten fish. The major you admire so much feels duty-bound to wash his hands after he takes our money to the bank.''

''I've noticed no such thing,'' Bao said.

''In which case, you are blind.''

The colonel stiffened slightly in his chair, behind the broad expanse of desk. ''Do not forget yourself,'' he said. ''Perhaps it's *your* attitude that prompts some men to treat you with disdain.''

Ling felt the anger burning in his cheeks, his stomach churning. Under different circumstances, he would happily have leaped across the desk to seize the colonel's throat and squeeze him until the light of life fled from his bulging eyes, but this wasn't the time or place for such a move.

''Of course,'' the colonel said, more gently now, ''there may be a certain truth in what you say. We have encountered racism before, not only from the white men in America and Europe. It isn't uncommon. It has seldom interfered with business, when the men who normally despise us are distracted by their bloated bank accounts.''

''This time is different,'' Ling insisted.

''Why?'' the colonel asked.

''Because they own this country. They aren't mere outlaws working in the shadows of the system, Colonel Bao. They are the system. What could be more logical than to accept your economic aid—and mine, in setting up the drug pipeline—and then betray us when the work is done, the project an established fact? We'd be in no position to complain or even to retaliate. Their friends in Washington would see to that.''

This time, the colonel frowned. ''And you believe the men responsible for your most recent losses are...who, exactly? The security police?''

Ling shrugged. ''Perhaps. They could as easily be members of the army or the death squads. It's impossible to separate the three, in any case.''

Bao hesitated for a moment, then replied, ''What is it you desire from me?''

Ling swallowed hard. His pride was bitter, going down. ''Permission to defend myself,'' he said.

The colonel made a small tent of his fingers, staring at their tips as if in meditation. Finally, he spoke. ''No man is called upon to let his foes destroy him without fighting back,'' he said, ''as long as he does not mistake true friends for enemies.''

''Of course,'' Ling said. ''My thanks.''

And he was smiling for the first time as he left Bao's office, heading off to give the remnants of his army marching orders.

''LOOKS LIKE we almost missed him,'' Bolan said, as Cruz pulled up and parked downrange from Ernesto Aguilar's stately home. The familiar stretch limo was parked in front, the trunk lid standing open. There were three guards at the curb making no attempt to hide their automatic weapons.

''The coward runs away,'' Cruz said, disdainfully. ''He loots our country, then expects to flee and pay no price.'' His hands were locked onto the steering wheel, his knuckles turning white from clenching.

''Too late,'' said Bolan. ''He's a day late and a dollar short.''

He had already switched the dome light off so there would be no giveaway glare as he stepped from the car. He had one foot out in the gutter when Cruz touched him lightly on the arm.

''You have the paint?''

''Right here,'' Bolan replied, patting the left-hand pocket of his coat.

''If anything goes wrong…''

"Then you know what to do," the Executioner reminded him, and stepped into the night, leaving the door ajar to forego any risk of noise.

The ritzy residential neighborhood was almost preternaturally quiet, no dogs barking, no sound of any kind emanating from the darkened homes that lined the street. Ernesto Aguilar's house was the only one showing lights at this hour of the morning, when the rich were still in bed after a long night of late dinners and club crawling. The only witnesses who concerned Bolan, were the three armed men beside the limousine, and any others who might be inside the house helping their master pack.

He closed the gap, cutting the distance in half with long strides, walking on grass to avoid the sound of scraping shoes on the pavement. The darkness and a weeping willow sheltered him when he was close enough to eavesdrop on the gunners' conversation. It was all in Spanish, Bolan picking up odd bits and pieces, but he heard enough to judge their attitude, deciding they were more or less relaxed, not worried that the shooters who were tearing up the town would pass this way.

So much the better, when he sprang his trap.

A male voice called out to the guards, from the house. The order was snapped out with enough authority to shut them up and spread them out a little, still remaining with the limousine. A moment later, Bolan saw a trio coming down the flagstone walk, Ernesto Aguilar sandwiched between another pair of guards. There were no spotters on the porch that he could see, no movement at the drapes in front.

So, call it six.

The Spectre submachine gun was already cocked and ready. Bolan let the new arrivals reach their destination, all six targets ranged along the sidewalk, one of the shooters bending down to open Aguilar's door. With all of them bunched that way, there was no point in picking out a special target. Bolan simply stepped from cover, braced the SMG against his hip, and hit them with a spray of Parabellum manglers from a range of twenty feet.

The Spectre has a cyclic rate of some 850 rounds per minute. Bolan fired off three-quarters of the 50-round magazine in just under three seconds, catching his targets flatfooted and dumping them together in a tangled heap of arms and legs. One of the shooters staggered clear and tried to make a break for it on rubber legs, but he was done, collapsing hard against the limousine and smearing it with blood on his way down.

Bolan removed the can of purple spray paint from his pocket, shook it several times as per instructions, stepping over twisted limbs as he moved closer to the car. He didn't read or write Chinese, but any symbol can be memorized, and this one was as fresh in Bolan's mind as if it had been tattooed on the inside of his eyelids. Working swiftly, confidently, he was finished in a moment, stepping back to view his handiwork. Bright purple over polished black, with dribbling streams of crimson for variety.

Not bad.

Cruz met him halfway, pulling forward, leaning out across the seat to open Bolan's door. "I hope Major Duende reads Chinese," he said, when they were rolling, well away from the shooting scene.

"He'll find someone who does," said Bolan. "We'll just have to wait and see what happens next."

"It's wrong, I know," Cruz told him, "but I really hate to stop."

"Who's stopping?" Bolan asked his friend. "We're on reconnaissance, that's all. A little watch and wait. The game's not over yet."

"I USED AN old man who sells opium without protection," Adolfo Quintana explained. "He didn't want to talk at first but I persuaded him."

"Enough congratulation of yourself," Major Duende snapped. "What does the damned thing mean?"

"It's the Chinese symbol—character, they call it—for revenge."

"Revenge?" Duende seemed both angry and confused, the mixture of emotions twisting his face into a strange half scowl. "Revenge for what, goddammit?"

It was Quintana's turn to make a face. "I'm not Chinese, *Jefé*," he said. "Who knows why they do anything?"

"They're businessmen," Duende said. "We know that much. They kill for money, power and to punish enemies. Revenge? For what?"

Quintana shrugged and looked around the all-night restaurant where Duende had agreed to meet him. With the major out of uniform and Quintana dressed down for the meeting, they resembled any other night-shift workers, winding down before they dragged their weary asses home to sleep. The death squad leader had two of his soldiers in another booth where they could watch the door, and two more in a car outside. Duende's plainclothes bodyguards were drinking coffee at the counter several yards away.

"I have it!" said Duende, leaning forward with his elbows on the table. "What if they thought we were responsible for the attacks they've suffered? They would certainly find some way to retaliate."

Quintana thought about it for a moment, then responded with a swift shake of his head. "It makes no sense," he said. "We've been in business with them since they first arrived in Panama. That's why they came here, *Jefé*. We have helped them kill the rebels who were stopping their narcotics shipments. Why would we attack them now?"

"They are suspicious people, these Chinese," Duende

said. "And proud, as well. They lose face if they don't react."

"And Aguilar? Why him? Why not come after you or me?"

"He made the deals," Duende said. "Responsibility was his, for failure or success. And for betrayal."

"So," Quintana said, "these monkeys are afraid of losing face? They'll lose a good deal more than that before I'm finished with them."

"Stop and think," the major cautioned him. "No great harm has been done, so far. We have a small misunderstanding, which can still be—"

"Small?" Quintana interrupted him. "The minister of commerce has been killed."

"He was, in fact, a simple deputy, and no great loss at that," Major Duende said. "We can retrieve this situation yet, Adolfo. I'm convinced of it. If I can only speak to Colonel Bao, perhaps to Ling, I'm sure that I can make them understand—"

Quintana never learned exactly what it was the major hoped to make them understand because the giant window opposite their booth chose that propitious moment to explode and shower them with sharp-edged broken glass.

BOLAN AND CRUZ had followed Major Duende from his home, guessing that anything that brought him out at that ungodly hour of the morning would involve a sit-down with potential targets and provide another opportunity for rattling their enemies. In Bolan's estimation, it would only take a few more acts of provocation to destroy the working coalition of Chinese and native thugs in Panama. He hoped so, anyway. If he was wrong, then all the blood and suffering had been in vain.

Bolan had thought Major Duende might be headed for his office, maybe even toward a showdown at the Chinese embassy, but Duende led them to an all-night eatery instead. Two bodyguards accompanied him inside and sat at the counter while Duende joined another, younger Hispanic man in one of the restaurant's booths.

"Adolfo Quintana," Cruz said, "in the flesh. Those men by the door are his soldiers. Also the two in the gray Ford over there."

"Okay, then," Bolan said, already scouting rooftops for a likely sniper's nest. "Turn right at the next intersection, and I'll walk back through the alley." He was counting doorways, gauging distance, so there would be no mistake.

"Where should I wait?" Cruz asked.

"Just make a two-block circuit," Bolan said. "Don't pass the restaurant again. You'll hear me."

"Yes, all right."

Cruz turned the corner and let him out. Bolan hiked back through the alley, counting shops until he found one with a metal ladder bolted to the wall for the convenience of repairmen. Topside, he removed the Walther WA-2000 from its duffel bag, chambered a Magnum round and found his position overlooking the diner.

Duende and Quintana seemed nearly life-sized in the eyepiece of his telescopic sight, lips moving urgently as they hunched forward, leaning toward each other over cups of steaming coffee. Bolan could have silenced them forever, but this still was not intended as an endgame move. The bodyguards, however, were another matter.

Six in all, and Bolan calculated that the two who had arrived with Duende would be plainclothes officers of the security police. He scratched them off his killing list, therefore, but there was nothing in the rules that said he couldn't scare them.

The Walther rifle held five rounds, and Bolan hoped that he would not need to reload. Speed and precision weren't mutually exclusive if a shooter knew his weapon, knew what he was doing well before he squeezed the trigger.

Bolan sighted on the two men in the booth close by the diner's entrance. Cruz had pegged them as Quintana's men, meaning they would be gunners for the death squad, both of them fair game. His angle wouldn't let him drill both targets with a single round, but their position facing one another in the booth meant he would only have to move a fraction of an inch between his first and second shots.

He sighted on a shaggy head, no face in view, drew in a deep breath, then released a part of it and held the rest. His index finger curled around the Walther's trigger, taking up the slack. Almost before the recoil of the first shot was absorbed, he shifted to the second mark—a face this time, still smiling at some comment from his friend—and fired again.

Bolan didn't wait to assess the impact of his shots. He swiveled toward the two plainclothesmen seated at the counter, caught them turning toward the sound of breaking glass and fixed his crosshairs on the plastic coffee urn between them on the counter. Round three scored a splash that scalded both cops where they sat and sent them diving for the floor in search of cover.

Bolan shifted once again and caught the last two gunners as they piled out of the car. One had a mini-Uzi in his fist; the other held some kind of nickel-plated semiauto pistol, probably a foreign knockoff of the old Colt .45. They scanned the street in search of targets, anxious to defend their master, but they never had a prayer.

Bolan lined up his shots and dropped them where they stood, a one-two punch so rapid that the twin reports reverberated through the night as one. Downrange, the ragdoll figures crumpled, hardware clattering on pavement as they sprawled in creeping pools of crimson.

Done.

He bagged the Walther, wasted no time getting off the roof and double-timing back along the alley, toward the street where Cruz had dropped him off. He waited thirty seconds for the rebel to arrive, and they were on the move again before the startled café manager recovered enough from his shock to summon the police.

"It went well?" Cruz inquired.

"We'll know soon," Bolan said. "You need to reach out to your contact with the cops once more and make sure we don't miss the main event."

13

Adolfo Quintana prided himself on his professional approach to homicide. He frequently despised the individuals his soldiers executed but he didn't allow his private feelings to dictate the actions of the death squad. Even now, when he had been humiliated in the public eye, four of his bodyguards cut down while he was cowering beneath a table praying to the Blessed Virgin for his life, Quintana wouldn't let his anger override the voice of common sense.

He had been trained in military tactics, after all, and knew that if he sent his men pell-mell against the Chinese Triads, even in their present weakened state, he would most certainly lose soldiers in the process, and he might risk another embarrassment.

It was essential that he plan each move and execute his plan precisely to avoid mistakes. To that end he had borrowed an idea of Duende's and had placed a call to David Ling, feigned penitence for any act that may have jeopardized the status quo between the Chinese Triads and the Panamanian regime. If they could only meet on neutral ground, he had suggested, there was no doubt they could put this sad unpleasantness behind them and continue earning cash, hand over fist.

He was relieved, though not especially surprised, when David Ling agreed.

The Triad would try to lay a trap, of course. Quintana was prepared for that. He couldn't say with any certainty how many Triad soldiers still remained in Panama, but they couldn't outnumber his own soldiers. Counting on brute force, if nothing else, to guarantee his victory, Quintana had summoned nearly a hundred members and close associates of the death squads. They were assembled that moment at a suburban warehouse, drawing arms from a truckload of weapons Major Duende had provided from the stockpile of the state security police.

It was Quintana's duty to motivate his soldiers, send them into battle with a sense of purpose that would carry them to victory. To that end, he must summon anger, patriotic fervor, racial prejudice and just the right amount of greed to make them see that risking everything they had, their very lives, was simply common sense.

Quintana climbed atop a stack of wooden forklift pallets, calling out for the attention of his soldiers. When they stood before him hushed and waiting, he regaled them with the story of the Chinese peril to their homeland. Asian gangsters had pretended interest in the well-being of Panama, Quintana said, and had seduced some members of the ruling junta into granting them extraordinary powers. Now, when they were close to domination of the country, they had gone back on their word, betrayed their oath of friendship and had spilled the blood of patriots. For what? To profit from narcotics and to gain advantage over the United States. It was an old, familiar story: Panama invaded, raped and looted by outsiders, while her people were forgotten, victimized. One of the patriots cut down that very night had been Ernesto Aguilar, a member of the presidential cabinet and friend of those who fought against corruption in the motherland.

The Chinese were tenacious, he explained, and while they, too, had suffered losses recently, they were well armed, well disciplined and still capable of wreaking havoc in the capital. He had arranged a meeting, but the Triad men would no doubt plot an ambush, scheming traitors that they were. Quintana was prepared for treachery, however, and had summoned his most trusted, most proficient warriors to assist him in disposing of their common enemy. When that momentous task had been accomplished, he suggested, those who stood behind him would share more than mere emotional rewards. There was a profit to be made, as well, and who deserved it more than gallant men who risked their lives for God and country?

Gratified by the applause that he received, Quintana beamed at his assembled soldiers, understanding that they trusted him and would obey his orders. He would lead them into battle personally, he proclaimed, and that drew more applause, together with a scattering of cheers.

It was, in fact, the very least that he could do.

He owed a debt of honor to the Triads, more specifically to David Ling, and meant to pay it off in blood.

CRUZ'S CONTACT with the state security police was nervous when he got the second call, but he came through with only minimal delay, returning Cruz's call after some fifteen minutes had passed. The rebel took it in a public phone booth, standing in the dark while Bolan waited in the car, holding his Steyr AUG with the Spectre submachine gun on the seat beside him.

Just in case.

The word was that Miguel Duende had been shaken by the sniper strike and something big was up, although the cops were being held back in reserve. Cruz's contact knew their destination—a soccer stadium in the southwest quadrant of the city—but he reported that police wouldn't be sent to smother the anticipated "riot" until they received a certain call. The way Cruz read it, Duende was unleashing his irregulars to clean house, holding back the men in uniform until they had a clear field and could be sent in to mop up stragglers without facing any major risk themselves.

Bolan agreed, and since Duende had no reason to suppose that he and Cruz would stop off for a predawn soccer game, it meant some kind of showdown had been scheduled with another enemy, most probably the Triads and/or Red Chinese. He guessed that Duende or Quintana would have made arrangements for a peaceful meeting, held on neutral ground, while planning how to stab their onetime allies in the back. The Chinese, for their part, were neither fools nor sitting ducks. However many guns they still had left in Panama, Bolan would cheerfully have bet that most of them were on their way right now to catch a hot, unscheduled soccer match.

Cruz knew the place and got them there in record time. The downtown traffic was already backing up, despite the hour, as another shift of workers found their way to jobs in factories, service stations, shops and restaurants. The downtown snarl was a delay, but nothing critical. Out toward the stadium, they seemed to have the residential streets all to themselves.

Bolan initially suggested that Cruz might be wise to simply drop him off, go back and tend to Vasquez's needs, but his companion stolidly refused. He wouldn't be left out when he had so much time and misery invested in the struggle. Bolan understood that feeling and he raised no further protest as Cruz parked the car a half mile from the soccer stadium and they began to walk back through the early morning darkness.

Getting in was relatively easy. Though the chain-link fence had curls of razor wire on top, the padlocked chains securing its gates were nothing special. Bolan found a gate that wasn't visible from passing autos and dropped the lock with two rounds from his Beretta. Once they were both inside, he draped the chain in place once more and tossed the lock away. It would be obvious if someone tried the gate, but there were also half a dozen other gates, four of them larger to accommodate the weekly crowds of boozy fans. Assuming someone used this gate, they would still have no way of knowing when the break-in had occurred or whether it had anything to do with the impending rumble.

Staking out positions in the stadium itself turned out to be the worst of it—at least, before the shooting actually started. There was no concealment to speak of in the bleachers, even lying prone, and once a sniper opened fire from that position he would be exposed to hostile gunners. The VIP box and announcer's booth way up on top had the best view available, but they were too far from the action. Bolan hadn't brought the Walther WA-2000 with him, and he didn't relish being trapped inside a glass-walled cubicle when several dozen gunners started firing on him.

That left them to seek positions closer to the playing field, a hundred-meter stretch of manicured grass marked off in chalk. The rough equivalent of bullpens were available on both sides of the field, and while they offered cover of a sort, the only way out in a pinch was to scramble topside into plain view of enemy guns.

He focused on the tunnels last of all. There seemed to be three kinds. One group of tunnels—eight in all, four on each side of the stadium—provided access to and from the bleachers for the paying fans; they also serviced snack bars, restrooms and the banks of public telephones. Another pair of tunnels, one on either side, led off to locker rooms and showers for the two opposing teams, positioned underneath the main bulk of the stadium. The final tunnel, situated near the northeast corner, was a solitary number, large enough to let a small truck pass. Bolan's companion told him that it served a maintenance garage and workshop for the grounds crew.

Bolan had a sudden inspiration, smiling as he spoke. "I'm checking out the maintenance garage," he said to Cruz. "If you want somewhere that they'll miss you coming in, smart money says they won't be passing through the shower rooms. Of course, I could be wrong."

"Don't worry," Cruz replied. "I have a place in mind." He forced a smile. "What is it that your movies sometimes say? 'See you in hell'?"

"Been there, done that," the Executioner replied. "We wrap this up, I'd settle for a nice cold beer."

"WE'RE LATE, goddammit!" David Ling turned sharply in his seat and glared at Michael Chan. "If those drivers live through this, I want their heads, you understand me?"

"Understood," Chan said. Two drivers chosen for the motorcade to the arena had been seven minutes late. They had arrived together, claiming some mechanical malfunction in their vehicles. Chan was surprised that Ling hadn't killed them on the spot.

Chan had already checked the stubby AKSU assault weapon resting in his lap, but now he took time to check it again, distracting himself from Ling's tirade. They had better things to think about than killing two drivers.

They were late. Ling was right about that. Not late for the meeting, which was still some twenty minutes off, but late for showing up ahead of their opponents, staking out the best positions in the stadium. Unless their adversaries were complete and total idiots, they would be well entrenched by now and waiting for the Triads to arrive.

We should have come an hour early, Chan repeated to himself, but who was he to countermand the orders of his master? He had suggested it, respectfully, and Ling had brushed him off. So be it. If they had to pay for Ling's mistake, Chan only hoped his own life wouldn't be a part of the price.

If something should happen to Ling, though, while the bullets were flying...

"Does something amuse you?" Ling challenged his second-in-command.

"Amuse me?" Chan was startled, raising his eyes from the weapon in his lap.

"Your smile, just now," Ling said, "was that of someone who enjoys a joke. Please share."

"There is no joke," Chan answered, willing himself not to sweat. "I simply look forward to killing these arrogant bastards."

"Ah." There was a hint of something—wariness?—in Ling's eyes, before he flashed a smile at the soldiers who shared his armored limousine. "You see, my children? That's the spirit! Every man must do his duty. Take no prisoners."

Chan thought of something, heard the jarring tone of it before he spoke, but knew he had to raise the question anyway. "Suppose they truly wish to talk, and nothing more?" he asked.

"It's too late," said Ling. "Their insults are unbearable. Aside from which, we have no further need of them. The drug routes are established, our agreement with the Cali is firm enough for now. The traffic to America and Canada won't be interrupted, even if we have to change the route a bit and ship through the Caribbean. I don't believe that it will come to that, however." David Ling was smiling as he added, "I have never met a Panamanian who wouldn't take a bribe."

They found the broad gates standing open when they reached the stadium, and after fleeting hesitation, they drove through and continued on inside. Four stretch limousines and one midsize sedan gave them seventy men, if Chan counted the drivers and Ling. He only hoped that it would be enough.

A single limousine was waiting for them on the track surrounding the soccer field, and Chan instantly wondered where the other cars were hidden, what had happened to the other men. The stadium was dark. For all he knew, an army could be lounging in the bleachers, weapons trained on the advancing motorcade.

"I don't like this," he said.

"You're not required to like it," Ling replied. "Just follow my instructions and we shall emerge victorious."

"Of course."

They parked some twenty paces from the waiting limousine and Chan stepped out. He held the AKSU down against his leg, concealing it as much as possible. It would require a nightscope for his enemies to see the gun, unless—

"Welcome!" an unfamiliar voice called out to him. "I'm happy you could join us. Let the games begin. Let there be light!"

The banks of floodlights mounted high above the soccer stadium blazed into life on cue, the sudden glare as blinding as a swift poke in the eyes. Chan physically recoiled, raising a hand to shield his eyes, and heard the same voice cry, "He's armed, the bastard! Fire! Fire! Fire!"

CROUCHING NEAR the entrance to the tunnel with the Thompson submachine gun braced across his knees, Cruz stayed alert to unexpected sounds from any source, either behind him or in front.

Quintana's men had reached the stadium eleven minutes after Cruz and Bolan had picked out their hiding places. Cruz had been relieved to see their caravan come in the normal way, through broad gates at the east end of the stadium. The vehicles were mostly black, and they unloaded swiftly, then retreated from the stadium as gunmen scattered through the bleachers. Cruz made ready to defend himself or flee, but no one chose his tunnel as a vantage point from which to watch the playing field.

The only vehicle remaining, once the motorcade retreated, was a single jet-black limousine. Its windows were so darkly tinted that he couldn't glimpse the occupants even in silhouette, or tell if they had lights on in the car. Cruz took small consolation from his knowledge that the vehicle was clearly bulletproof, in any case, and it would do no earthly good for him to see or recognize the men inside.

A hissing, crackling static somewhere overhead told Cruz the gunners were communicating with some kind of two-way radios, no doubt receiving orders from the limousine. And he didn't require a formal course in military strategy to understand their aim. Whoever drove or walked into the soccer stadium from that point on would be entering a target range. And they would be the targets.

Cruz appreciated the professional approach to killing off one's enemies. He had employed the same technique himself, though on a smaller scale, when he was leading raids against the drug convoys in the Serrania del Darién. If he had only had more men and guns, he thought, perhaps some of the soldiers who had followed him would be alive today.

Another sixteen minutes slipped away before he heard the sound of vehicles approaching. Cruz couldn't have said how many. He simply watched and waited, crouching in the darkness, wondering if the American had found something in the maintenance garage to help them even out the odds. It seemed unlikely. Still...

The first of four stretch limousines pulled into view, the stately caravan advancing cautiously. The fifth and last car in the line, a black sedan, looked puny by comparison.

Cruz watched the limos and sedan pull up a few yards from the waiting vehicle, their lights and engines switching off. Doors opened simultaneously on the Quintana limousine and on the point car for the Triad motorcade. A Spanish-sounding voice—Quintana's?—called out to the Chinese team, "Welcome! I'm happy you could join us. Let the games begin. Let there be light!"

Cruz flinched as every floodlight in the stadium blazed on, turning the soccer field as bright as noontime on a summer day. He saw the Chinese beside the limousine raise one arm to protect his eyes and heard the other man—it was Quintana, Cruz could see him now—shout to his troops, "He's armed, the bastard! Fire! Fire! Fire!"

There was no hesitation from Quintana's gunmen in the bleachers and the dugouts. Something like a hundred weapons opened as one, full automatic, shotguns, semiautomatics, pouring fire into the limousines and black sedan. The one man who had stepped out of the point car went down instantly. Cruz reckoned he was dead before he hit the dirt.

The echo of that raging gunfire in the tunnel almost deafened Cruz, but it could help him, too. No one among Quintana's soldiers would suspect he was an enemy, unless he fired on them directly. It was even possible they wouldn't notice him at all, as caught up as they were in pouring fire into the Triad vehicles.

The motorcade was taking hits, but of the five vehicles on the track, only the last in line, the black sedan, was compromised by the incoming fire. The limousines were armor plated, Cruz saw now, with bulletproof glass and self-sealing tires. Already, they were jockeying for new positions, muzzle-flashes spitting from gun ports along both sides of each limo. Incoming bullets chipped paint from the bodywork, baring bright steel underneath, but none of the fire seemed to penetrate metal or glass.

The tail car was a different story, though. Its occupants were dead or dying now, their car riddled and settling on four flat tires as dark fluid streamed from the punctured radiator. Cruz could only wonder what possessed them to drive in that way, without protection from their waiting enemies. Nothing he felt for them would pass for pity or remorse.

Cruz put the dead men out of mind entirely in another moment, concentrating on the battleground outside and his best angle of attack. Guillermo Cruz had come to play, and he was not about to let the best part of the action pass him by.

"NOT YET," Major Miguel Duende said into the mouthpiece of his two-way radio. "Hold your positions. Anyone who moves without my order will be placed under arrest and held for court-martial."

He sat and listened to the sound of gunfire from a block away. How many guns? The echoes from the soccer stadium made it impossible to say, precisely, but there was a major firefight under way. Quintana, in their final conversation, had suggested he might take as many as a hundred men to face the Triads, making sure he had an edge. How many soldiers did the Chinese have, meanwhile? The last count, prior to all this bloody trouble, had been something like 150 fighting men in Panama at large, but who could really say? At least four dozen had been killed or wounded in the latest series of attacks around the capital, and he had watched the Triad motorcade as it approached the stadium, judging that even if the four stretch limousines were crammed with seventeen or eighteen men apiece, the black sedan with six, Quintana should still have his enemies outnumbered.

Should have.

Duende was displeased with the uncertainty of it. For all he knew, the Triads might have reinforcements waiting in reserve somewhere close by, prepared to close the pincers at a signal from their men inside the stadium. Or, then again, suppose that Colonel Bao Bai-fan had decided to join the struggle, supporting his countrymen. Then what? How many of the Chinese "tourists" presently in Panama were really members of the People's Army, waiting for an order to attack their hosts, perhaps to seize the capital itself?

Such a bizarre conspiracy wouldn't succeed, Major Duende realized. The gringos from *El Norte* would step in to rout the Chinese threat, if it came to that, but any such development would come too late for Duende, much too late to salvage his career. As the commander of the state security police, he was supposed to know of such things in advance, weed out subversives or at least warn his superiors of danger in the offing. Should it come to all-out fighting in the streets with the Chinese, Major Duende would be doomed, no matter which side won the fight. In fact, he knew, he would be lucky to avoid a firing squad.

Quintana had been promised all the time he needed to destroy the Triads. Duende had intended to stand by and wait until the death squad leader's signal told him it was clear to move in with his troops, mop up the stragglers and accept the credit for crushing a seditious conspiracy.

Now Duende was experiencing a dramatic change of heart. He reached for the microphone again, pressed down the transmitter button with his thumb and barked an order to his waiting troops.

"All right!" he snapped. "We've waited long enough! Remember who your targets are and follow me!"

He didn't say, Kill only the Chinese. That part was understood by every man selected for this mission, each of them from captains down to privates briefed in varying detail. They understood that certain foreign enemies had lured loyal, law-abiding patriots into a death trap at the stadium. The patriots would certainly defend themselves as best they could, but it was always possible that they might not prevail. Whatever happened, every man in Duende's strike force would remember that his enemies tonight were Asians, more specifically Chinese.

And each man would remember the injunction to be merciless, to take no prisoners.

Quintana drew his pistol as the staff car started moving toward the stadium, encroaching on the battleground. He wondered whether he would be alive to see the sunrise, tried to offer up a prayer, but couldn't think of anything to say.

No matter.

God was doubtless busy at the moment anyway with all these new arrivals to be judged, before He flushed them down to Hell.

14

Bolan had made good use of his half hour in the maintenance garage before all hell broke loose out in the stadium. The grounds crew had two pickup trucks besides the riding mowers and assorted other gear. He would have liked to use the telescoping crane somehow—for novelty, if nothing else—but he could think of no way to deploy it that wouldn't have marked him as a hopeless sitting duck.

Instead, he found a sledgehammer and smashed the safety glass out of the newer pickup—windshield, driver's window, all around. He swept the broken glass out of the driver's seat and heard it crunching under foot as he retrieved a welder's torch and mask, together with some strips of sheet metal. The sheets were six feet long, ten inches wide, and Bolan's torch cut through them as if they were made of plastic, trimming them to fit his needs. Once he was finished, he started welding them across the empty windows of the pickup's cab, leaving himself a view port where the open sides and windshield used to be, with nothing in back.

He would have liked to do the grille, as well, but he was out of time. Bolan couldn't make out the words when someone started shouting from the stadium, but there was no mistaking the barrage of gunfire that erupted seconds later. When he slid behind the pickup's steering wheel and slammed the door, he knew it wasn't much, as tanks go, but it was the best he could prepare on such short notice.

It would have to do.

He turned the engine over, put the truck in gear and rumbled out of the garage. His first glimpse of the stadium since he had parted company with Cruz almost dismayed him. There were gunmen in the bleachers on both sides and in the dugouts, pouring fire into four limousines and a sedan, the smaller car already out of action, dead on the track. The limos were fighting back, spitting gunfire and maneuvering off-track onto the grass. Whether they meant to run or stand and shoot it out was anybody's guess, but Bolan had a few plans of his own.

He hit the track at twenty miles per hour, gunned it up to forty on the straightaway and started watching for targets. No one knew exactly what to make of him, at first. He was approaching the rear end of the stationary limo when three shooters tried to intercept him, breaking from the dugout on his left and charging into his path.

It wasn't much, as plans went, and he ran two of them down before they had a chance to dodge the pickup, still apparently believing he would stop. The third man leaped aside and fired a submachine-gun burst as Bolan passed. A couple of his bullets struck the metal plates welded across the driver's window, denting them, before they ricocheted into the night.

So far, so good.

The truck wasn't an armored vehicle, of course, and any kind of concentrated fire would ultimately stop it dead. Stop him, as well, for that matter. The Executioner knew all these things, and he didn't intend to die behind the wheel if there was viable alternative. He still had speed, firepower, some maneuverability and a dwindling measure of surprise on his side.

With any luck at all, he thought, it just might be enough.

And if it wasn't...

Bolan swung the wheel hard to his left, jolted across the

asphalt curb that separated dusty track from well-kept grass and took off in pursuit of a retreating limousine.

ADOLFO QUINTANA flinched involuntarily when his armored limo started taking hits. He craned forward in his seat, cursing as four of the five Triad vehicles began to maneuver through the plunging cross fire, muzzle-flashes blazing from their gun ports. He began to imagine the cost of failure, of letting the Chinese slip away from him with only six or seven of them killed when he had laid the perfect trap. None of the leaders had been hit so far, Quintana reckoned, and they wouldn't be, as long as they remained inside the armored limousines.

He had a sudden, reckless thought of how to save the situation and make himself a hero in the process. One bold stroke could turn the game around, Quintana thought. There was a risk involved, of course. If not, there would be no reward awaiting him, should he succeed.

Before he had a chance to falter, he moved forward past the huddled gunmen, shouting at his driver. "You! Martinez! Ram the lead car! Quickly, before it gets away!"

Martinez didn't hesitate. He knew who paid his salary and who could make his death an endless, screaming nightmare if he faltered under fire. The limousine surged forward, bumped across the asphalt curve and gained momentum as its tires found purchase on the grass. Quintana toppled over backward, landing on his ass, but none among his soldiers dared to laugh at him. A moment later, he was on his hands and knees, peering across the driver's shoulder through the tinted windshield.

They were catching up, no doubt about it. Even in a tank like this, Martinez was a race driver at heart. The second Triad limousine swung out and tried to block them, but Martinez brushed it off, metal rending as they scraped past and left the blocker in their wake.

It would accomplish nothing, as Quintana saw it now, to simply ram the Triad limo from behind. A case of whiplash for the Chinese, perhaps, but otherwise, the tap would simply speed them on their way.

"Swing out and take them from the side!" he told the driver urgently. "They must not leave the stadium!"

Gaining speed, Martinez swung the steering wheel hard left and veered off course, then brought it back until they were running parallel with the Triad limousine. Still trailing, they would need more speed if they were going to catch up. Martinez found it somewhere, mashing the accelerator to the floor, and while the tank was never meant for hot pursuit, it was designed for hasty exits under fire.

Another moment, and they pulled abreast of the Triad vehicle, bullets hammering Quintana's limousine before his men started shooting back through starboard gun ports. Yet another moment, and they had begun to pull ahead, but Martinez swung the steering wheel back sharply to the left and cried, "Hang on!"

Quintana braced himself for impact. With two such heavy vehicles, it bore no physical resemblance to a car crash in the movies. It was more like sumo wrestling, or a head-butting contest between elephants. Quintana lost his balance again, but caught himself with an outstretched hand before he belly flopped. Some of his gunners were down on their knees, faces pressed against bulletproof glass and shouting curses at the enemy.

The Triad limousine was slowing, swerving back in the direction of the bleachers where his snipers were. The unseen driver tried to fight it, but he couldn't overcome the laws of physics. In another moment, they would hit the track again, and then—

The sudden glare of high beams through the tinted windshield startled Quintana. What were these vehicles arriving so late on the scene? Why did they look so strange?

Quintana quickly realized that they were military vehicles, and that an armored car—a minitank, in fact—was leading them. He didn't know all of the nomenclature, but he recognized the 20 mm cannon that protruded from its turret.

Christ! Major Duende had decided not to wait! What was the crazy bastard thinking? How could he execute the plan they had agreed on, with his people simply mopping up, when there had been no resolution of the conflict yet? How could Quintana's soldiers slip away without exposure if the stadium was already surrounded?

"Idiot!" Quintana said, to no one in particular. He tried to focus on the Triad limousine, picturing David Ling behind the smoked glass, face twisted in a grimace of fear. If only he had some way to breach the other limo's armor, he could—

Suddenly, it hit him. He had been provided with a radio, a walkie-talkie tuned to the security police frequency, for use in alerting Duende's men when the battle was over. Now, if he was quick enough, it still might work to his advantage.

Scrambling back to get the radio, Quintana switched it on and started jabbering into the mouthpiece. "You, inside the tank! There are two limousines in front of you. The Triad leaders are inside the limo to the left!"

He watched the turret start to swivel, following the limos as they kept grinding and scraping toward the bleachers. He could see the 20 mm cannon lining up on target and immediately recognized his fatal error.

"No!" he howled into the walkie-talkie. "Wait! Your left! Your—"

Quintana saw the muzzle-flash and closed his eyes, unable to watch as the world exploded in his face.

GUILLERMO CRUZ was up and moving when the armored limousine exploded. Close beside it, the second limo was spattered with burning oil and gasoline, apparently unable to break free, their bumpers locked or some such thing. He saw the doors pop open, armed men spilling out onto the track searching for cover as the gunfire all around them somehow managed to intensify.

Cruz didn't know why the security police had changed their plan, but he was glad to see them in the thick of things. Their presence caused confusion and distracted Cruz's enemies. It might even help the American—who else could it be racing around the soccer field in some kind of converted pickup truck and spraying automatic fire at soldiers of both sides?—but Cruz wasn't convinced of that.

Someone inside the armored car that led the train of military vehicles had seen Bolan's pickup zigzagging erratically across the grass. Cruz saw the turret tracking, heard the loud *bang* of the cannon, then witnessed its first shot miss, the HE round exploding in the bleachers. Through the smoke, Cruz saw an airborne body tumbling back to earth, but if the sniper screamed, his voice was lost in the explosion.

There was nothing Cruz could do to help Bolan, and he kept his head down, checking out the military convoy, searching for a target he could reach. These men, or others like them, had annihilated dozens of his friends barely twelve hours earlier. Cruz hated the security police more than the Triads and the death squad murderers combined. The others were all criminals, and recognized as such, whether their crimes were ever punished in the courts or not. These men in uniform, by contrast, had been sworn in with an oath to uphold and enforce the law, which made them murderers and hypocrites. If Cruz could only find—

He blinked, at first convinced that wishful thinking had deceived him, painting Major Duende's face on someone else. Cruz had to look a second time before he recognized the truth. The major had seen fit to supervise the action personally from the front seat of a military staff car. As he rolled along the track, between two armored personnel carriers, Duende surveyed the battlefield like a conquering hero, as if he were invincible.

Bulletproof glass in the car? No, the windows were down! Duende's arrogance had given Cruz the opening he craved, his one best chance.

Leaping across the rail, he landed on the dirt track in a fighting crouch. No one appeared to see him coming as he ran toward the staff car, reaching out to rest the muzzle of his Thompson submachine gun on the windowsill. "For liberty, Duende!" he declared, and held down the Tommy's trigger.

Cruz gave them half the drum, perhaps a little more, Miguel Duende twitched in his seat as .45 slugs ripped his uniform to bloody tatters. There was no resistance from the others, in their shock, but Cruz was spotted as he stepped back from the car. The APC behind the staff car swung out and rumbled toward him as he started to retreat.

Too late Cruz thought about escape and realized there was none to be had. His last twenty rounds or so were wasted on the APC's armor, but Cruz didn't care. He pictured Ariana Vasquez in his mind and he was smiling when the .30-caliber machine gun cut him down.

BOLAN HADN'T EXPECTED military intervention in the middle of the firefight, but he saw that it could work to his advantage—that is, assuming that he could remain alive and dodge the 20 mm cannon rounds that chased his homemade APC across the soccer field.

Each miss so far had served to scatter, wound or kill his enemies. Two HE rounds had gone off in the bleachers, flinging bodies through the air like rag dolls, and a third had detonated on the track, among some running men who were eviscerated and dismembered by the blast. He didn't know or care which side had suffered more, since both camps were his adversaries, and he wished them both the very worst of luck.

Another 20 mm round exploded, close enough to jar the pickup this time, and he heard its shrapnel ripping through the truck's sheet-metal bodywork. The gunner was about to drop one in his lap, if Bolan didn't take some steps to throw him off his game.

The best defense, he knew, was still a good offense. With that in mind, he swung the pickup's steering wheel around and brought it into a collision course, aimed head-on toward the minitank. With any luck it would surprise the gunner just enough to make him hesitate before he fired. All Bolan really needed was a second, maybe two.

He stomped on the accelerator, felt the pickup's rear wheels digging in and had one hand on the door handle as a sudden surge of speed shoved him back in his seat. An image flashed across his mind, the door jamming tight, an old clip from *Rebel Without a Cause*—but it worked perfectly, Bolan grabbing for his Steyr AUG as he spilled from the driver's seat onto the grass.

The pickup kept going on a straight-arrow course. The 20 mm cannon fired once more, its HE round punching through his makeshift windshield armor, detonating in the cab with force enough to peel the roof back, turning it into an instant convertible. The shot was high and it didn't stop the truck from plunging forward, slamming hard into the tank. At the same time the armored vehicle was also moving, and its treads began to climb the pickup's bumper, grille, across the hood, crushing the truck...until it got stuck.

Glancing back, he saw the tank crew bailing out, as flames began to blossom from the pickup's ruptured fuel tank. Bolan left them to it, briefly counting heads and reckoning that three would be the minitank's full crew. If they got shot by someone else while they were wandering around the soccer field, it wasn't his fault. He had still maintained his promise not to kill a cop.

He found Guillermo Cruz a moment later, where the APC had rumbled over him. Its giant tires had missed the body, but machine-gun fire had done the job intended. Several paces away, Bolan saw the staff car, stalled and motionless. He recognized Miguel Duende slumped in the back seat, his uniform more crimson than khaki.

Rough justice.

The death of their commander had apparently unhinged Duende's troops and scuttled any plans they had for favoring one side over the other in this fight. The APCs were raking stands and field alike with their machine guns now, and soldiers were unloading from the vehicles, adding their small-arms fire to the cacophony.

It struck Bolan that they were doing his work for him, mopping up both sides. A second armored car had plugged the exit from the stadium, its 20 mm cannon blasting at the last two limousines in motion, scoring a decisive hit on one of them as Bolan watched. The HE round punched through a window that was advertised as bulletproof by manufacturers who never counted on that kind of firepower. When it exploded in the passenger compartment of the jet-black stretch, it blew out the other tinted windows, bright tongues of fire licking the night.

Bolan was looking for an exit, homing in on the tunnel leading to the nearest locker room, when he picked out a figure ducking in ahead of him. The floodlights told him there was no mistake.

Bolan was on the trail of David Ling.

The tunnel echoed with his target's running footsteps, Bolan taking care to make less noise in his pursuit. He reached the locker room and showers seconds after Ling and glimpsed his quarry making for the lighted sign that marked an exit to the world outside. Players slipped out that way sometimes when they had lost the game and were embarrassed to confront their disappointed fans.

"That's far enough, Ling!" Bolan called across the room. "End of the road."

Instead of risking a rush toward the exit, the Triad leader stopped and turned to face him. Even winded, worried, with his face blood-dappled from a scalp wound, Ling still hung on to a measure of his dignity.

"You are American?"

"In case it matters," Bolan said.

"What do you want with me?"

"Think of me as the your worst nightmare," he replied. "You should have stayed at home."

"I have no home," Ling said. "The Communists have stolen it, and now America tells me I can't settle here."

"You're not a settler," Bolan told him, edging closer. "You're a parasite."

Ling shrugged, his left arm heavier, some kind of stubby automatic weapon in his hand. "I fill a need," he said. "Your people crave the powders. I meet their demand."

"Past tense," the Executioner corrected him.

Ling smiled. "When dealing with Americans," he said, "I always find your arrogance refreshing. You waste no time on the hollow courtesy my people find obligatory. I admire the way you—what's the phrase?—ah yes, cut to the chase."

"This *is* the chase," said Bolan.

"So it is."

Ling was a swift, efficient shooter, but he telegraphed his move by tilting slightly to the right, his shoulder dropping half an inch or so, bracing to swing his weapon up and fire a long one-handed burst. Bolan was there ahead of him, the AUG unloading from a range of less than twenty feet.

He stroked the trigger twice, two 3-round bursts, watching the 5.56 mm tumblers rip Ling's chest and abdomen. The Triad leader, dead before he fell, still managed to unleash a burst of wild fire as he toppled over backward, bullets rattling into empty lockers, chipping paint and cement from the walls.

There was no need to check to see if Ling was still alive. The brief exchange of gunfire had been covered by the racket from the stadium, but even that was fading now, the firefight trailing off. Bolan didn't have time to stand around and guess who would emerge victorious. The winners, or the next wave of police, would soon be searching high and low for any stragglers at the scene, and something told him the authorities wouldn't be taking prisoners.

It was high time for him to leave.

And the Executioner still had work to do.

Epilogue

Colonel Bao Bai-fan was going home. It wasn't his idea—the order had come through to the embassy that morning—but he was pleased to know that he would soon be out of Panama, perhaps for good. It had gone sour on him here, as no mission had ever done before, and Colonel Bao was sickened by the bitter taste of failure, even as he felt relief at getting out alive.

There would be questions in Beijing, of course. His various superiors wouldn't be pleased by late developments. Indeed, his very summons home was proof of that. Still, Bao believed he could explain what had gone wrong—his own role in the mess, at least—and lay the blame where it belonged, on profiteers and criminals, perhaps with some assistance from the CIA. If all else failed, it never hurt to wave Old Glory in the faces of the men who held the reins in China. Even with most-favored nation trading status from the USA, suspicion still ran deep with die-hard Communists, and any difficulty could be traced to Washington, if one tried hard enough.

The colonel checked his Rolex, pleased to know the car would be outside in moments, ready for a quick trip to the Chinese embassy. Bao wouldn't bother cleaning out his desk, since he kept nothing there of any consequence. His files were under lock and key, waiting for his successor to pick up where Bao left off, or else to shred them and pretend that nothing ever happened. In the alternate scenario, there were no drugs, no tentative alliance with the Triads or Colombians, no evidence of any criminal activity traceable to citizens of the People's Republic. Whatever libel might be published in the Western press, Beijing could still claim ignorance and innocence.

Bao finished packing, latched his solitary suitcase and was waiting when the limousine pulled up outside. He waited for his escorts to step out, approach the house and ring his doorbell. All four of them wore the proper badges, marking them as members of the Chinese diplomatic team, immune from any interference by the Panamanian authorities.

All was as it should be.

Bao left his bag for someone else to carry, opening the door. He didn't smile, since pleasantry was wasted on subordinates. These men expected nothing from him and they would receive precisely that. The only reason they existed was to see him safely from his home to the embassy, and on from there to the airport. They would never be his friends. In fact, Bao thought, he had no memory of seeing them before.

The first alarm bell rang inside his head. How could that be? The Chinese embassy in Panama wasn't a crowded place, and while Bao didn't socialize with underlings he knew the staff by sight. Who were these men? Why were they reaching underneath their jackets?

Recognition of the truth arrived too late for Colonel Bao Bai-fan. He turned to run, already knowing it was hopeless, as the massed fire of four machine pistols struck him like a dropkick to the spine, propelling him forward, spilling him across a sofa that toppled over backward from his weight.

He never saw or heard the leader of the hit team step around behind the couch, bracing his MAC-10 Ingram in a firm two-handed grip. "For David Ling," the shooter said, and emptied out the stubby weapon's magazine.

"I WON'T ASK if he was brave. This, I already know."

Her eyes were red from weeping, but her voice was steady. Bolan had explained the circumstances of Guillermo Cruz's death, exaggerating only slightly when he sketched the toll Cruz had exacted from their enemies. Major Duende was enough, all by himself, to guarantee a hero's memory.

"Yes," Bolan said, although she hadn't asked him. "He was brave."

"I'm still not sure I understand about the Chinese colonel, though," she said. "Did you...?"

She was afraid to ask if Bolan had assassinated Colonel Bao Bai-fan.

"I made a phone call to the Triads," he explained, "and told them Colonel Bao betrayed their brothers to the death squad for a personal advantage. It was something they could understand. They did the rest."

She nodded, seeming pleased. There was no tremor in her voice as she went on. "And you are finished now in Panama."

"I've done my part," he said. "The rest belongs to patriots like you. There's no compelling reason why you can't promote a decent government, without some outsider dictating every move."

"You say strange things, for an American," she said, and forced a smile.

"I'm not exactly standard issue," Bolan said, responding with a warm smile of his own. "I know it won't be easy, Ariana, but you've got a fighting chance, here, and the scandal won't do anything to help the junta, when you think about it."

"They've been scandalized before," she said. "I just

don't know if we can do it, Mike. I mean, we've never really had an independent government in Panama. First Spain, then the United States, now the Chinese and the Colombians.''

"You don't strike me as someone who gives up when things get tough," he said.

"Guillermo didn't either," she replied. "Where has it gotten him?"

"He went down fighting," Bolan said, "and he took out the chief of the security police."

"I shouldn't have described what Duende did, when I…'' She hesitated, on the verge of breaking down again. "It's my fault, isn't it?"

"You're not to blame for any crimes committed by your enemies," Bolan replied. "They'd love for you to think that way. It ties you up in knots and you go crazy, punishing yourself."

She studied him through eyes brimming with tears. "Are you so hardened, then? Do you feel nothing?"

"What I feel and what I do," the Executioner informed her, "are two different things. Each time you go to war, you run a risk of losing things and people that you care about. It happens, and there's no avoiding it. You mourn, and you go on. When mourning takes up all your time, becomes the only thing you think of, you're as good as dead. You may as well lie down and let them shovel in the dirt."

"So, you are hard and wise," she said. The smile was back, still tentative, but stronger.

"It's a funny thing," he told her. "Wisdom's almost inescapable, if you survive and learn from your mistakes."

"I hope you're right." She paused, then asked, "Will you come back to Panama sometime, and see if I've grown wise?"

"Stranger things have happened," Bolan said. "You never know."

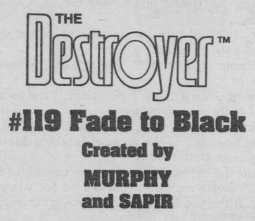

Take
2 explosive books
plus a
mystery bonus
FREE

JAMES AXLER

DEATH LANDS®

Pandora's Redoubt

Ryan Cawdor and his fellow survivalists emerge in a
redoubt in which they discover a sleek superarmored
personnel carrier bristling with weapons from predark
days. As the companions leave the redoubt, a sudden
beeping makes them realize why the builders were
constructing a supermachine in the first place.